The Kite
Fighters

OTHER DELL YEARLING BOOKS YOU WILL ENJOY:

SEESAW GIRL, *Linda Sue Park*

YANG THE YOUNGEST AND HIS TERRIBLE EAR
Lensey Namioka

YANG THE THIRD AND HER IMPOSSIBLE FAMILY
Lensey Namioka

YANG THE SECOND AND HER SECRET ADMIRERS
Lensey Namioka

YANG THE ELDEST AND HIS ODD JOBS, *Lensey Namioka*

YEAR OF IMPOSSIBLE GOODBYES, *Sook Nyul Choi*

ECHOES OF THE WHITE GIRAFFE, *Sook Nyul Choi*

SING FOR YOUR FATHER, SU PHAN
Stella Pevsner and Fay Tang

AKIKO ON THE PLANET SMOO, *Mark Crilley*

AKIKO IN THE SPRUBLY ISLANDS, *Mark Crilley*

The Kite Fighters

by LINDA SUE PARK

Decorations by EUNG WON PARK

A Dell Yearling Book

35 Years of Exceptional Reading

Dell Yearling Books
Established 1966

Published by
Dell Yearling
an imprint of
Random House Children's Books
a division of Random House, Inc.
1540 Broadway
New York, New York 10036

Text copyright © 2000 by Linda Sue Park
Illustrations copyright © 2000 by Eung Won Park
The illustrations for this book were executed in pen and ink.

Visit us on the Web! www.randomhouse.com/kids

Educators and librarians, for a variety of teaching tools, visit us at
www.randomhouse.com/teachers

ISBN: 0-440-41813-5

Reprinted by arrangement with Clarion Books

Printed in the United States of America

February 2002

10 9 8 7 6 5 4 3

CWO

This one is for Ben.

Acknowledgments

I am grateful to David Gomberg, whose assistance regarding the technical aspects of kite flying and fighting was invaluable. Any errors that remain are mine.

Marsha Hayles and Joan and Kevin Lownds read the manuscript of this book and offered many helpful suggestions. I thank my agent, Ginger Knowlton, for her acumen and support.

My greatest thanks to my editor, Dinah Stevenson, and always, to my family—to Sean and Anna, the best first readers a writer could ask for, and to Ben, my biggest fan.

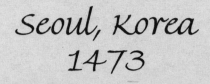

Seoul, Korea
1473

chapter one

Young-sup watched as his older brother, Kee-sup, ran down the hill with the kite trailing behind him. The kite bumped and skittered along the ground, but if Kee-sup got up enough speed, it sometimes caught a low puff of wind and rose into the air.

Sometimes.

Not very often.

Every tenth try or so.

In the air the kite would hold steady for several moments, then dive without warning. Kee-sup ran in different directions, pulling desperately on the line, but to no avail. The kite always ended up on the ground with its twin "feet" crumpled beneath it, looking, Young-sup thought, both angry and ashamed.

Young-sup watched silently. He did not bother to

ask for a turn; Kee-sup would offer when he was ready. It was his kite, after all.

Kee-sup had been given the kite as a birthday present several days before, as part of the New Year celebration. The New Year was everyone's birthday. It didn't matter on which date you were born; you added a year to your age at the New Year holiday.

Young-sup's gift had been a *yut* set. Normally, he would have been delighted to receive the popular board game, with its little carved men. But when they opened their gifts, his first feeling was one of envy.

His brother's kite was wonderful. It had been purchased from Kite Seller Chung, who made the finest kites in the marketplace. Two huge eyes were painted on it, to help it see its way clear into the skies; heavy eyebrows made it look fierce and determined. Young-sup had to swallow hard to hold back his jealous words.

It hadn't helped that Kee-sup had left immediately to fly the kite on his own. Young-sup had begged and pleaded and pestered for days, and today, at last, Kee-sup had invited him to the hillside to fly.

The snow-dusted hill on which the brothers stood stretched down toward the great wall that surrounded Seoul. The road that wound around the base of the hill led to one of the city's nine enormous gates. Beyond the wall Young-sup could see hundreds of rooftops, huddled together and crouched low to the ground, as if bowing to the palace at the center of the city. The grand tiled roofs of the royal palace stood out in graceful curved splendor. No other structure was permitted to rise higher.

Young-sup continued watching in silence as the kite took yet another dive and crashed. At last Kee-sup handed it over. Young-sup felt a river of eagerness surge through him as he took it.

He had decided to try a different technique. Holding the kite at arm's length in one hand and the reel in the other, he threw the kite up into the air.

It came straight down and would have hit him on the head if he hadn't dodged out of the way.

"I tried that before," said Kee-sup. "A hundred times. It never works."

Young-sup picked up the kite. In that brief moment he had felt why it would not fly.

On only his second try he launched the kite from a complete standstill.

Kee-sup's jaw dropped. "Hey! How did you do that?"

Young-sup shrugged, not wanting to display too much pride. "I'll show you," he said. For he knew in his bones that he could do it again.

The kite flew proudly. Young-sup let it play for a

few moments, thrilled at the pull on the line in his hands. Bringing in an arm's length of line, he experimented, plying it to and fro. The kite made graceful figure eights, swooping and dipping like a playful fish. Then Young-sup reeled in, keeping control until the kite floated just overhead. He gave the line a final, gentle tweak, and the kite drifted to the ground.

Young-sup picked it up and began to demonstrate. "First, you let out some line, not too much but enough to give it a little slack." Holding the middle of the kite in one hand with his arm outstretched, he turned his body slightly. "Then you must stand with the strength of the wind at your back, and hold the kite like so. There will come a moment when the wind is just right. That's when you throw the kite into the air and allow it to take up the extra line."

Young-sup waited a few moments. Then, as if obeying his words, the kite leaped and rose to stretch the line taut. It was as if an invisible hand had pulled the kite into the air.

He brought it down again and handed Kee-sup the reel. "Now you try."

Kee-sup arranged the line and held the kite as Young-sup had done, then released it and yanked on the reel. The kite crashed to the ground.

"No, no!" cried Young-sup. "The most important thing is to wait for the right moment."

"How do you know when it's right?" Kee-sup sounded cross.

Young-sup hesitated. "It's right when it—when it . . . Can't you tell?"

"Of course not. That's why I'm asking you, pig-brain."

Young-sup tapped his chin lightly with his fist, thinking. Then he scanned the ground around his feet until he found a slim stick. He used it to draw in the powdery snow—a crude sun, a few clouds, a tree. "Look," he said. "If you could draw the wind, what would it look like?" He gave the stick to his brother.

"What do you mean? Wind doesn't *look* like anything."

"Just try."

Kee-sup hesitated, then added a few curving lines to the landscape.

"That's right." Young-sup nodded. "That's what I see when I fly a kite."

"You can't *see* wind."

"I know, I know. But you can *feel* it, right? And you can see what it does."

"The way it moves the trees."

"Yes, the trees . . . but it was more than that."

Young-sup spoke slowly, trying to find the right words. "I could tell what the wind is like because the kite—" He glanced at his brother, lowered his eyes, and mumbled, "The kite talked to me."

"The kite *talked* to you?"

"Yes," Young-sup answered, more sure of himself now. "The first time, when I tried throwing it into the air, something said to me, 'More—more line' and 'Wait . . . wait for the wind. . . . *Now!*' It must have been the kite. What else could it be?"

Kee-sup frowned for a moment. Then he laughed suddenly and slapped his knee. "The kite must have a *tok-gabi!*"

*Tok-gabi*s were invisible imps who visited every household from time to time. When the rice burned or an ink pot spilled, such incidents were blamed on a *tok-gabi*. They were mischievous spirits but seldom caused real harm. Young-sup joined his brother in laughter at the thought of a little imp clinging to the kite.

"Perhaps you have somehow angered the *tok-gabi*," Young-sup joked.

"Well, one thing is certain," Kee-sup said. "Whatever language kites speak, I haven't learned it yet."

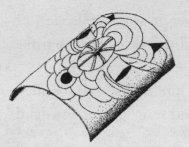

chapter two

The boys put the New Year kite away when spring arrived; kite flying was considered a winter sport. They spent the warm days playing other games. Now, with summer fading and the days growing shorter, both brothers were thinking of kites again. Kee-sup began to make a new one.

Young-sup thought it a good thing that his brother had found his way from flying a kite to making one. The seeing kite was well worn. Kee-sup's bumpy launching technique had often knocked the wooden frame askew. Loose sticks and rocks had torn the paper. Kee-sup had spent as much time patching and repairing as flying.

Clever with his hands, Kee-sup had made many toys in the past: bamboo dolls for their two little sisters, boats to sail on the Han River, a whole collection of carved animals. Hearing of his brother's plan to make a kite, Young-sup decided to make one as well.

It was high time he had a kite of his own. Besides, a kite was only a few sticks and some paper; how hard could it be to make one?

....

Young-sup watched as Kee-sup used a length of line to measure the bamboo sticks.

"Why do you need to do that? Look, mine are already cut. I'm ready to glue and tie them now."

Kee-sup was using the seeing kite as a model. He took his time, ensuring that the frame for the kite he was making matched the first one in every way. Meanwhile, Young-sup had moved on to the kite paper. He guessed at where the center of the rectangle lay and cut a rather lopsided circle out of the middle.

Kee-sup shook his head. "It's crooked."

"So what?" Young-sup shrugged. "You need a hole in the middle for the wind to blow through—it doesn't matter if it doesn't look nice." Young-sup felt the same way about decorations for his kite—plain white paper suited him fine. He didn't have time to waste on decorations. The important thing was to get the kite into the air.

As it turned out, he had to wait anyway. Kee-sup would not lend him the reel and line until his own kite was ready. And Kee-sup took the longest time over the decorations for his kite.

He drew little sketches of his ideas and made miniature kites out of folded paper. These tiny versions, dozens of them, were lined up on a shelf in the boys' room.

The graceful feathers of a crane. A leopard's countless spots. Bold Chinese picture words like "Luck," "Heaven," "Happiness"—the intricate Chinese symbols were considered more poetic than their Korean counterparts. "That one's good," Young-sup would say, trying to keep the impatience from his voice. "Why don't you choose that?" Kee-sup would only shake his head and fold the paper for yet another little kite.

Finally he chose a tiger design. Then he made half a dozen little tiger kites, experimenting with different patterns of stripes. Young-sup thought he would go mad with the itch of waiting.

It was several more days before the tiger was ready— the longest wait of Young-sup's life. At last the time came for the four-leg bridle of line to be attached to the frame. When Kee-sup tied the final knot, Young-sup couldn't stop himself from whooping with delight.

....

The next day the brothers headed out to the hillside for the first time that season. Though each now had his own kite, they still had only one reel between them. Young-sup begged so hard to be the first to use it that Kee-sup finally gave in, and together they tied the reel to the plain white kite.

Young-sup launched confidently. But the kite bucked and kicked and crashed unceremoniously after only a few moments in the air. Young-sup frowned and tried again. This time the kite stayed in the air, but it refused to obey the line's commands; indeed, it was only his superior skill that enabled the kite to fly at all.

A few moments later the kite plummeted to earth in a most undignified crash. Kee-sup trotted toward it. Over his shoulder he grinned and called, "It looks as if the *tok-gabi* is angry at *you* now."

Young-sup scowled. "That's not funny." He reached for the offending kite. But Kee-sup held it away from him, inspecting it carefully.

"Look—your crosspieces aren't the same length,"

he pointed out. He held the kite in both hands, pushing one side and pulling the other; with very little effort, the frame twisted crazily. "And the whole frame is unstable. That's why you're having so much trouble."

Young-sup sulked, but he knew his brother was right. "Let me have a turn with yours," he begged.

"Yes, all right. But I want to fly it first."

They untied the reel from Young-sup's kite and attached it to the tiger. Kee-sup stood at the top of the hill and fussed with the kite for a few moments, adjusting the line and reel. Finally he looked at Young-sup.

"I don't want this one to get bumped and torn like the seeing kite. Help me launch."

A launch was easier with two people. Young-sup held the kite and Kee-sup the reel. Young-sup released the tiger at the right moment, then watched as it soared into the air, sure and true, as if all tigers could fly.

....

Young-sup loved the feeling of a kite on a line. He liked the moment of launching when he stood perfectly still, feeling the wind at his back and the kite's desire to be in the air. He experimented constantly, teasing the line this way and that, holding the reel different ways, even turning his whole body at varied angles, to coax the kite into following his commands.

The wind was always his partner, one he must strive to understand with the kite's help. Sometimes it was like a kitten, pawing gently at the kite, nudging it across the sky. At other times it was a big dog, friendly and eager but too rough in its play. It would bat and swipe and seem to shake the kite in its jaws.

On many occasions the wind died completely. At those moments Young-sup could feel the line slacken just before the kite began to fall. A lightning reaction, where his hands reeled in almost before his mind had finished the thought, would find a freshet of wind in another patch of the sky. Other times he discovered that the only way to stop a kite's fall was to give it *more* line, not less.

The kite was like a part of him—the part that could fly.

....

With the failure of his own homemade kite, Young-sup was forced to borrow his brother's tiger when he wanted to fly. Kee-sup was willing enough to share, for he had given up altogether trying to learn to launch a kite on his own. Either his lack of skill or the naughty *tok-gabi* made his kite crash every time. Young-sup now helped with each launch, and Kee-sup repaid the favor by allowing him to have a turn with the tiger.

Despite plenty of opportunities to fly, Young-sup was not content. More than anything he wanted a good kite of his own. One afternoon as they walked home from the hillside, he silenced his pride and spoke. The words did not come easily.

"Brother, I was—I was truly a failure at making a kite. You made yours so well. Would you make one for me?" He hesitated, then went on. "It would be such fun to be able to fly together instead of taking turns. And the tiger is magnificent. It would be a great honor to fly one just like it."

Kee-sup walked on, looking down at the ground, and did not answer for a few moments.

"No," he said finally.

Young-sup opened his mouth to protest. Kee-sup held up his hand for silence, then halted there in the road to speak.

"I won't make one for you. But I'll *help* you make one of your own. You must make the frame, but I'll do the decorations for you, so it will look just the same."

In a rush of relief and eagerness, Young-sup agreed. But Kee-sup had one more thing to say.

"This time you must build the frame exactly as I tell you. A kite like your last one is just a waste of time. If you want a kite worthy of a tiger's stripes, its bones must be strong."

....

The work was painstaking from the very start. Kee-sup insisted that Young-sup measure the bamboo sticks precisely. The first time, Young-sup was careless with the measuring string. He pulled it taut for one stick but less so for the second. After he had cut the sticks, he found that they were uneven. Kee-sup made him measure and cut them again.

If the knife slipped the merest hair, it was enough to make the sticks uneven. "Cut them again," Kee-sup ordered.

Time after time Young-sup had to clench his teeth so the words of frustration would not escape. But as the days went by, the kite's construction gained his interest. He began to see that the flying walked invisibly beside every step of the making.

"I know that you can see the wind and I can't," Kee-sup said jokingly, "but we both know what it's like—how strong it can be. The frame must be just as strong."

Young-sup nodded. He knew the thrill of seeing how light sticks of bamboo and mere paper could be the wind's equal.

The angles and corners where the sticks met received critical attention. Kee-sup showed him how these were the most vulnerable points. If time and care were not taken on the joints, the first stress of the wind against the paper could misalign them. The smashed grains of cooked rice they used for glue were messy and seemed to get everywhere. Often Young-sup found that his very fingertips were stuck together.

Even the simple bridle was a lesson. "The points where you attach the line must be placed so," Kee-sup explained. "If it is fixed to one side or the other—even a little—the balance will be wrong. The line will pull harder on one side."

"I felt that with my first kite," Young-sup admitted.

Bit by bit the frame was completed. Then Kee-sup turned his attention to the paper. Young-sup was delighted as the work progressed. Kee-sup was making the pattern of stripes subtly different from his own tiger kite, so that the kites looked similar but not the same.

Like brothers.

chapter three

The boys had to halt work on the kite for a few days. A soothsayer had been consulted and had chosen a propitious day for Kee-sup's capping ceremony. The boys' mother kept them busy with a hundred different chores to prepare for this important rite.

On the day chosen by the soothsayer, the family dressed in their finest clothes and assembled in the largest room of the house—the Hall of Ancestors. The room sparkled with cleanliness. Porcelain vases of fresh flowers brought bright spots of color to each corner. The finest scrolls had been hung. And the tempting smell of the food for the celebration feast drifted through the whole house.

Kee-sup knelt in front of his father, who then untied

the silk cord that held the boy's hair in a single long braid. Kee-sup's hair was unbraided, and a little hair oil was smoothed into it. Then his father combed the hair upward, tugging and pulling the comb through the tangles.

Young-sup watched closely. He had never seen a capping ceremony before. He thought it must hurt Kee-sup whenever the comb was yanked free. But not once did he flinch or wince, and Young-sup wondered if he would be able to be as stoic when the time came for his own capping ceremony.

Kee-sup's hair was twisted upward and around itself until it formed a smooth knot on top of his head. The topknot was tied firmly in place with silk thread.

Kee-sup rose to his feet and turned to face his father. On the low table before them lay a finely woven horsehair cap. His father placed the cap carefully over Kee-sup's topknot and tied the silk ribbon under his chin. It was a plain narrow ribbon, such as those worn by the unmarried or by ordinary men. Semiprecious stones or silver beads on the ribbon indicated a family man of substance and wealth; the chin strap of the boys' father was strung with coral beads.

Then Kee-sup bowed to his father, a formal ceremonial bow, all the way to the floor on his knees. He rose and went to stand before the stone ancestral tablets. Bowing again, he thus honored the spirits of his ancestors.

The formal bows took a long time; Young-sup's thoughts drifted like a leaf on the water. He wondered how things would be different for Kee-sup after today. Some things, he knew, would be just the same. He sighed inwardly, thinking of the trips up the mountain.

Several times a year his father, as the eldest son of his family, made the journey to the mountainside gravesite of his ancestors. There, a ceremony was held to honor their spirits. Four years ago, when Kee-sup passed his tenth New Year, he had begun making the trip as well.

Watching Kee-sup make his bows now, Young-sup felt a flicker of anger, though he was careful to keep it from showing on his face. *It's not fair,* he thought. *I've passed eleven New Years already. Why can't I go?*

The most recent trip had taken place in the last moon, as part of the festivities for the Great Autumn Feast. Young-sup had summoned his nerve on that day and asked his father for permission to join the worship party. "Perhaps next time" was the reply.

Young-sup had been forced yet again to imagine what the trip was like. One might see a tiger, or a bear, or at least a deer. There might be secret caves to explore. And surely there would be big trees to climb— bigger than those that grew around the city. Young-sup knew that there was a lovely stream near the gravesite; Kee-sup had told him about picnicking there.

And Kee-sup hadn't even wanted to go! At the time he had been hard at work on his tiger kite. Young-sup recalled his brother's sullen face as he left for the trip. It was beyond understanding—Kee-sup could work on his kite any day. A trip to the mountains was special.

....

The capping ceremony was not yet concluded. On the table lay a new jacket of white linen. The boys' mother had spent many hours sewing nearly invisible stitches into the fine, closely woven fabric.

Kee-sup shed his grass-green jacket, and his father helped him into the new one. Children wore bright colors; when a boy became a man, he donned the white clothes of adulthood. His father tied the ribbon at the front of the jacket in a one-loop bow, and Kee-sup's transformation was complete.

His father faced the rest of the family, with Kee-sup by his side.

"See my first-born son!" he announced. "Today he is a man."

Young-sup rose with his mother and sisters. All of them bowed down low to show respect for Kee-sup's new position.

The capping ceremony was symbolic of a young man's readiness for marriage; in fact, many families included it as part of the wedding ritual. As Young-sup knelt with his forehead low, he considered why their father had chosen this moment for Kee-sup to be capped. It was probably a way of reminding him of his upcoming responsibilities. Young-sup knew that the thought of the royal examinations was never far from their father's mind.

....

After the celebration meal the boys crossed the courtyard together. Young-sup kept glancing at his brother.

"What is it?" Kee-sup asked finally, annoyed.

"Nothing." Young-sup giggled. "You just look different in that cap, that's all."

"Ha! Well, you'll be getting one in a few years

yourself, you know. And stop laughing at me. You're supposed to show respect now."

"I know, elder brother. But if you think I'm going to be bowing to you all the time, you can just forget it."

Kee-sup bellowed in mock anger and chased him into their room.

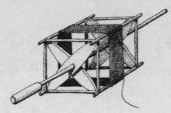

chapter four

With his own tiger kite nearly finished, Young-sup faced another problem. He needed a reel and line.

Kee-sup's reel had come with the seeing kite. Both brothers thought that perhaps Kee-sup could make a basic reel, but the best reels were more than simple spools. In skilled hands, they were designed to let out or bring in line quicker than the eye could follow. Only a craftsman could precisely position the spindles for the correct balance, and such labor commanded a high price. In addition to the reel, Young-sup would need line, and good silk line was costly.

Young-sup went first to his father and asked him for the money to buy a reel and line.

His father frowned—as Young-sup had known he

would. "Borrow your brother's reel, my son. He should be spending more time at his studies anyway. Perhaps next year you can have one of your own."

The refusal was disappointing but not unexpected. Young-sup had been fairly sure that he would have to think of another way.

Could he save the money? On the days when he and Kee-sup went to the marketplace, his father always gave them a few *won* to buy sweets. But a good kite reel cost many *won*. Young-sup calculated . . . months, perhaps. He added the figures again and shook his head angrily. It would be close to a year before he could save enough. He wanted a reel *now*.

Young-sup had been quiet for several days, trying to think of a solution. One afternoon his mother called to him.

"Your face is like a month of rain, my son," she teased gently. "What makes the clouds inside your head so dark and heavy?"

Like most Korean women, the boys' mother governed the household. With the help of one maidservant, she planned and prepared the meals, did the laundry, and cleaned the house. It was she who ordered the purchases of food, clothing, and other supplies. But, following tradition, she herself never left the house—nor handled money. Her husband would give Hwang, the manservant, whatever money was necessary to do the shopping.

So Young-sup knew that his mother would not be able to help him and that even if she had the money, she could not go against her husband's wishes. But the problem seemed too great for him on his own, and he found himself confiding in her.

"I can't ask Elder Brother for his reel all the time, Mother. And besides, my kite is nearly finished. We each need our own reel."

She looked at him for a long moment. "I'm sorry, my son. But you must not walk around with your head down all the time. Who knows? If an answer were to fall from the sky, you would never see it!"

For her sake Young-sup tried to smile. An answer from the sky. If only it were that easy.

....

Young-sup fingered the few coins on a string in his pocket. They were not even one-tenth of what he needed for a good reel, but he could not resist strolling by Kite Seller Chung's stall while his father and brother spent the afternoon doing various errands.

Just to look, Young-sup said to himself. He knew

which reel he wanted. It was gleaming wood, wound with the finest silk line. He stared at it, stroked it gently, finally picked it up and held it. He imagined what it would feel like to have such a fine reel in his hand with his kite dancing at the end of the line . . .

"You choose well, young one." The kite seller's words broke into his thoughts. "That is one of my finest reels."

Young-sup nodded wordlessly. He put the reel down and turned away, his thoughts still full of kite and wind and sky.

Almost without thinking he looked up. It was a beautiful late-autumn day, perfect for kite flying. The wind was just right. *That reel should be mine*, he thought. *If the old kite seller could only see me fly, he would see that I deserve such a reel.*

Suddenly Young-sup turned back to the kite seller's stall. An idea had come to him all at once, a foolish, impossible idea. But why not? What had he to lose?

"Honorable sir!" he called to the kite seller. "How is your business today?"

The kite seller shrugged. "The New Year is still months away—people have not yet begun to buy kites for the holiday. My best season is not quite upon me."

"How would you like it to begin today?"

The man laughed. "What are you saying, son of Lee? Do you have a way to make the New Year come more quickly?"

"No, but I do have a way to make more people buy your kites."

The kite seller raised his eyebrows. "My ears are open."

"If I were to fly a kite right here, in front of your stall, people would see it—even people far away. On such a fine day it would give many the idea of flying a kite . . . and they would come to you to buy them."

The kite seller was silent for a few moments. Then he spoke. "Your plan has not one but two weak legs. First, there is not enough space in front of my stall to fly a kite. And second, even if there were, I am thinking that such service is not being offered for my thanks alone."

Young-sup bowed his head in respect. "The honorable kite seller is right in his second thought. I do wish to be paid—but not in money. And as to the first, I can fly a kite anywhere."

Surprise wrote itself on the man's face, for Young-sup's words were not spoken in a voice of idle boasting. "Just say that you *could* do it. How would you be paid, if not in *won?*"

Young-sup's eyes darted to the reel, then back to the kite seller's face. He did not speak.

"Oh-ho! So you think this service worth the price of the reel?" The kite seller spoke with both challenge and respect in his voice.

"How many kites would you think to sell today?" Young-sup asked.

"Today? Two, perhaps three. What are you thinking now, little flier?"

Young-sup took a deep breath. "I will fly a kite here. If you sell five kites today, the reel is mine."

The man countered with another offer. "For such a fine reel, *seven* kites. But that is not all. I see you do not have a kite with you, so you must use one of mine. If you damage it—no reel. *And* you must pay for the kite."

Young-sup bowed, and Kite Seller Chung returned the bow. The bargain had been made.

....

The market stalls had been set up in two rows, with a space between them for customers and foot traffic. The space was perhaps five paces wide. Young-sup would have to fly the kite in the small area in front of the kite stall. To stray in front of another stall would perhaps anger its owner.

Luck was with him that day; the wind blew down the length of the market, rather than across it, where its strength would have been blocked by the stalls. Young-sup took up the kite and reel offered him by the kite seller and stood still, as he always did, feeling for the wind.

The kite seller watched as the kite rose effortlessly. He did not smile, but if Young-sup had looked behind him, he would have seen the man's slow nod of admiration.

....

It took all of Young-sup's skill to control the kite within the confines of the space in front of the stall, but as time went on, he grew more accustomed to its limits. It seemed an eternity before the first kite was sold.

A man stopped in front of the stall, watched the kite for a little while, then bought one. His spirits renewed, Young-sup found that he could perform some of his favorite maneuvers. The kite's loops and twirls attracted more attention—and more customers.

The afternoon passed slowly; a second kite was purchased an hour after the first. By now much of the marketplace had heard of the bargain. A circle of onlookers gathered, watching to see whether Young-sup would win the reel.

Two soldiers watched the flying demonstration for a while, and one of them bought a kite. He teased and cajoled his friend into buying one as well. And the little audience cheered when another man stepped up to the stall and bought not one but *two* kites.

The sun slanted low over the market stalls. Young-sup's heart sank. It was time to go—and only six kites had been sold.

"The time is gone, young flier," the kite seller called. "I must close the stall and go home."

Young-sup bowed his head. Then he looked up at the kite again. *I did my best,* he thought. *What more can I do?* And he turned his attention to the final task: getting the kite down safely.

He played the line carefully, guiding the kite toward the narrow space between the stalls. Just a little more line to be reeled in now . . .

Behind him he heard quick footsteps. Then the magic words: "A kite, please, Honorable Kite Seller!"

Young-sup's heart leaped in his chest. He dared not turn around, as the kite was just now passing between the stalls. It floated gently down to earth before him. Quickly he reeled in the remaining line, picked up the kite, and turned back toward the stall.

A small boy in dirty, ragged clothes was pointing

to one of the kites. The kite seller looked dubious. "Show me the money, urchin," he demanded.

Defiantly the boy opened his palm and displayed a string full of *won*—more than enough for the kite he had chosen. The kite seller shrugged, took down the kite, and handed it to him. Joy shone in the child's face, and he dashed off again, disappearing beyond the crowd.

The kite seller reached for the precious reel and held it forth in his two hands.

"Well earned, flier," he said, and bowed.

Young-sup bowed in return. He exchanged the kite he had been using for the reel, and for a brief moment the eyes of the man and the boy met. The look they exchanged spoke of their love of flying; no more words were needed.

Young-sup looked around and saw his father and brother waiting at the edge of the marketplace. He walked toward them through the crowd, which was buzzing with the news of his accomplishment. Some of the people shouted or smiled as he passed, but he kept his head low and the reel at his side, for to display it or to acknowledge their praise would have been considered boastful.

Winning the reel was reward enough.

chapter five

Young-sup dashed up the hill with his kite, at last attached to the shining reel. He waited impatiently for Kee-sup to join him.

As usual Young-sup helped his brother launch. Then he released his own tiger. For the first time the two striped kites flew side by side.

Both boys shouted with glee. Young-sup thought it was the finest thing he had ever done or seen—his tiger kite in the sky with the hard-earned reel in his hands. The brothers ran about the hillside until they were breathless. Then they stood and flew more quietly for a while, until Young-sup felt rested. He began running again, this time roaring like a tiger. Kee-sup joined in.

"Tigers forever!"

"Tigers rule the sky!"

A stern shout interrupted their roars. "Ho, you! On the ground when the King approaches!"

The two boys turned in amazement to see a soldier approaching them. The King? What was he talking about?

A few years before, His Majesty the King had died suddenly. The custom and law of the land dictated that his son become King in his place. That was the natural order of things.

Except that the son had been only eight years old.

It was the boy's mother, the Dowager Queen, who ruled the country now with the help of many advisers. She would continue to do so until the young King reached the age of manhood. Meanwhile the boy did not govern. But he was still King.

Young-sup and Kee-sup knew all this; they had even seen the boy-King when he was paraded through the streets of Seoul after his father's funeral. They remembered his solemn round face peeping through the trappings of his regally draped palanquin. They knew, too, that he was close to their age. But in that enormous palace, walled off from the city and guarded by soldiers, he seemed almost a creature from another world.

And now, here he was, on their hillside.

....

As the royal palanquin was lowered to the ground by the King's attendants, the brothers reacted at once as dutiful subjects. They knelt and touched their foreheads to the ground, to remain so until the King ordered them to rise.

But because of the kites, their bows were rather . . . untraditional.

When Kee-sup went to his knees, he dropped his reel. At once it skipped across the ground, as the wind-aided kite dragged it along. Doubled over in an otherwise proper bow, Kee-sup twisted his neck in an effort to see where the reel was headed.

Young-sup tightened his grip on the smooth wood of his precious new reel—not for a million *won* would he have risked its being scratched or scarred. Instead, he knelt with the reel held straight out to the side, to prevent the line from getting tangled about his body.

He hoped fervently that he did not appear disrespectful, but his extended arm felt as conspicuous as a giant red flag. Out of the corner of his eye he could see Kee-sup trying to catch a glimpse of his reel, and he knew that neither of their bows was perfectly correct. What would the King think? What if he were displeased—what would he say or do?

"Rise," the King commanded. Both boys stood up, keeping their heads bowed, but Young-sup stole a quick peek at His Majesty's face beyond the partially opened curtains of the palanquin. It was difficult to tell, but the King did not appear to be angry.

"So," he said. "It is you who hold the leashes of the tigers. I saw them from my garden."

Kee-sup answered. "Yes, Your Majesty."

"Ha!" The King gave a sudden shout of laughter and pointed at Kee-sup's reel. "You must make haste to catch it before it escapes!"

Kee-sup turned to go after the reel, turned back to the King, hastily bowed his head, and then ran down the hill.

But the reel had too great a head start, and Kee-sup could not catch it. The King turned to his guards. "You four! Assist him in the task!" The guards bowed their heads, then charged off in pursuit of the runaway reel.

Young-sup was not sure if he, too, should join in the chase. But he still held his own reel, and he glanced at it now. He knew that if all the line should pay out, it would be difficult to reel in again. Did he have to ask the King's permission to get his kite under control?

He looked up to see his brother and the four guards some distance away. Just as they drew near the reel and stooped to grab it, it hopped and jerked out of their reach. The five figures looked as though they were performing a very strange dance, bending, stooping, straightening, and skipping to the beat of unheard music.

The King began to laugh. "Ah—it eludes them yet again!" he exclaimed. "It would seem that the reel does not wish to be captured!"

Young-sup swallowed a smile. He was not sure of the correct behavior; was he allowed to laugh in front of the King?

Finally one of the guards pounced on the reel and held it up in triumph. The King applauded in delight as the guard handed it to Kee-sup. Then the little group made their way back up the hillside, with Kee-sup reeling in his kite as he walked.

The King looked skyward again. Young-sup's kite had taken up nearly all his line and was so far away that its stripes could no longer be distinguished.

"Bring it closer," the King commanded. Young-sup immediately began the careful process of reeling in the kite. He manipulated the reel to draw in the line a little at a time. It could not simply be wound in continuously; if Young-sup did not take care to read the wind, the kite might take a sudden dive when it was still very far away.

Young-sup brought the kite in until its stripes showed proudly again. Then he turned to the King and bowed his head.

"Would Your Majesty like to hold the reel?"

The King jumped out of the palanquin. Now that His Majesty was standing, Young-sup could see that they were about the same height. The King wore a heavily embroidered scarlet silk gown and an elaborate jeweled cap.

He took the reel without even replying. Young-sup saw the look of delight on his face; he knew the feeling well.

A few sticks, a little paper, some string. And the wind.

Kite magic.

chapter six

Young-sup watched helplessly as Kee-sup tore yet another miniature kite to pieces and threw it savagely on the pile of crumpled paper at his side.

At the end of their encounter with the King, His Majesty had issued a royal command.

"Make me a kite—a King's kite. Bring it to the palace when it is finished. The guards will let you in." One of the men with the King—not a guard, since he was not dressed as one, perhaps a royal adviser—had suggested that any number of kites could be purchased for the King at the marketplace. But the King was adamant. Not just any kite would do; he wanted a kite that would fly like Young-sup's tiger.

The brothers had walked home from the hillside in silence. As they approached their home, Young-sup finally spoke. "You will make him a kite, of course. But it may not fly as mine does."

Kee-sup nodded wordlessly. Young-sup saw the thoughtful expression on his brother's face and tried to imagine what it would be like to serve the King with his own two hands.

....

What could it possibly look like—a King's kite? Young-sup suggested another tiger, but Kee-sup shook his head at once.

"It would not be right, brother, for the King to have the same kite as we do. It would be almost . . . an insult." And Young-sup could see how this would be so.

He felt useless as Kee-sup struggled in an agony of indecision, producing model after model. No design that he drew seemed good enough.

The boys had told their father of meeting the King, and though the elder Lee rarely showed emotion, it was clear that the news impressed him. He had freed Kee-sup from his usual studies for as long as it would take to build the kite.

The frame was completed first. Kee-sup took extra pains with it, of course, but with the experience of the two tiger kites behind him, its quality was assured. It was the design that was the problem—and time was passing quickly. The King had not mentioned a deadline, but both boys felt it would be disrespectful for Kee-sup to take too long.

Finally, after dozens of tiny paper kites had been made and rejected, the brothers consulted their father—and wished they had done so from the first.

Their father had answered at once. "A dragon, my son. Our country's symbol for His Majesty."

A dragon! Of course! Young-sup knew at once that his brother could do it. It would be beautiful—truly fit for a King.

The whole family had a role in the endeavor. Young-sup helped by fetching supplies; he would sometimes stay to talk a little, or just to sit and watch. Their mother kept the little sisters away from the room so Kee-sup could work. Their father bought two rolls of the finest-quality rice paper. He, too, stopped by the boys' room from time to time to check on the kite's progress.

At last the sheet of paper was complete. The brothers stood side by side and surveyed the work critically.

The paper was indeed beautiful. Dozens of identical red scales covered it. Each scale overlapped its neighbor, and the rows of scales overlapped one another in perfect, symmetrical rhythm. Every scale was outlined in black.

"You've done it, brother! It will make a wonderful kite!"

Kee-sup knit his brows, and for a fleeting moment Young-sup thought how much he looked like their father. "What's the matter? Aren't you pleased with your work?"

Kee-sup shook his head. "It's good, I know. But it's still not quite right—something's missing."

"What do you mean? It's amazing! All you have to do now is fit it onto the frame. Not even Kite Seller Chung has made such a kite as this!"

"It's still not right. I don't know exactly what it is . . . " Kee-sup's voice trailed off.

Young-sup felt a familiar impatience at his brother's artistic scruples.

Two days later Kee-sup was still refusing to cut the paper. Arguing over it yet again that evening, the brothers looked up in surprise and bowed hastily when their father entered the room.

He frowned at Young-sup. "You were arguing with your older brother," he said.

"Father, I was only trying to express that it would be disrespectful to keep the King waiting—"

Shaking his head abruptly, his father cut off Young-sup's words. "Your brother has been capped. He is no longer a boy. You must not forget this. You cannot quarrel with him as if he were a puppy. You will not treat him so discourteously again."

Young-sup kept his head bowed throughout his father's speech, as was proper when accepting a reprimand. He fought to keep his face blank, even as his throat tightened with the feeling of injustice. *It's just a hat*, he thought rebelliously.

Kee-sup cleared his throat. "Father. I have worked hard. I find the design very good. But—" He hesitated.

"Something is missing."

"Yes."

Silence again. Then, "Sleep now, my son. Perhaps morning will bring you an answer."

Young-sup felt a fleeting curiosity; he knew his father well enough to know that nothing he said was ever without a reason. But the wondering soon left his mind as other thoughts seemed to fill up the darkness. He tossed about, unable to sleep.

Kee-sup is my brother, the same as he has always been. But now, somehow, I'm supposed to treat him differently. After spending what seemed like half the night in restless thought, Young-sup decided to speak respectfully to

Kee-sup when they were around others—especially their father.

Sternly he told himself that he had to try, for nothing would change the fact that Kee-sup had been born first.

....

The boys' father was known in his work as Rice Merchant Lee. The farmers whose rice he bought respected him because although he demanded the highest quality from them, he treated them fairly. And his customers knew that their rice would always be white and pure, without stones or leaves or other debris to pad out the bags' weight or bulk.

So he was able to provide a good living for his family. But long years in the business had taught him caution. One year of drought or flood would mean hard times for the farmers and for himself. Lee was not a stingy man, but always he watched his earnings carefully.

The greatest part of his income was spent on hiring the best tutor he could afford. The tutor came to the house every day to give his sons lessons. Lee's plan was for Kee-sup to enter the King's court as a scholar. It was such men—those with much learning and education—who were held in the highest esteem in society.

Entry to the court was by examination. The examinations were held every three years, and Kee-sup would be taking them in the next cycle. Lee saw to it that the boy studied hard, for the examinations were extremely difficult. Only those with the best scores earned places at the court.

As for Young-sup, perhaps one day he would take over the rice business. Lee loved both his sons, but the family honor was dependent on his first-born. This was the custom, the age-old tradition.

There was no other way.

....

The next day, after the evening meal, the boys' father came to their room. He held out a little parcel. As Young-sup looked on, Kee-sup opened the paper wrapping to discover a small ceramic jar.

As always their father was a man of few words. "Gold leaf," he said.

"Gold leaf?" Kee-sup echoed.

"Paint. With real gold in it."

Young-sup understood in the same moment as his brother. "For the King's kite," they said in unison.

"Yes. Now go finish." Their father left the room then, but not before both boys had seen the shadow of a smile cross his face.

....

"Outline each scale in gold, brother. That would look very impressive."

Kee-sup shook his head. "I thought of that already. There isn't enough."

"Well, what about a little spot in the center of each scale? That would look good, too."

"But such a small spot might not show up well from a distance." Kee-sup frowned at the dragon paper, deep in thought.

Young-sup scowled. He was doing his best to help, but Kee-sup was rejecting every suggestion he made. He tried one last time. "How about a Chinese picture word painted in gold? You could write 'Royal dragon' or something like that. Something that tells of its whole character, its whole—whole . . . I can't think of the right word, but do you know what I mean?"

Kee-sup looked up suddenly. "What did you just say?"

Young-sup sighed in exasperation. "Weren't you listening? I said to paint a Chinese word—"

"No, no, not that part. The part about showing its whole character."

"Oh. I just meant, we should think of something that shows its whole . . . essence—that's what I was trying to think of before."

Kee-sup clapped his hands in excitement. "That's it, brother! You've done it!"

Young-sup grinned. "You like the idea? What word do you think would be best?"

"I'm not going to paint a word, brother." Young-sup's face fell. "But never mind—you've given me an idea. Now I just need to work out how to do it." And though Young-sup pestered him all throughout the day, he would say no more.

....

Even when Kee-sup finally declared that he knew how he would use the gold leaf, still he delayed. Each day Young-sup would ask if today was the day to finish the kite paper, and each day Kee-sup would have an excuse—he was too tired because he hadn't slept well, or he wanted to think about his idea one more time. Several more days passed.

The evening meal was finished, and the boys were in their room. Their father's shadow fell across the doorway. He glanced at the painted paper on the shelf, still red and black, as it had been for days, then looked at Kee-sup.

"The paint is gold. Not magic. It will not paint the kite by itself." And he turned away as quickly as he had come.

The boys looked at each other. Young-sup felt a pang of sympathy for his brother. All the same he knew their father was right.

"Enough delay, brother." Young-sup spoke gently. "You can do it—no one better. It's time, you know."

Kee-sup nodded without a word.

Young-sup spread a linen drop cloth on the floor and took the dragon paper down from the shelf. Kee-sup opened the jar of gold leaf carefully. He picked out a rabbit-hair brush, then spoke. "I need the knife, too."

"The knife?"

"The one we use for kite making, to cut the bamboo sticks. Fetch it from Hwang for me."

"All right, but why—"

"No questions," Kee-sup said firmly. "And when you bring it back, I want to work on this alone."

Young-sup did not argue. The King's kite was of greater importance than his own curiosity.

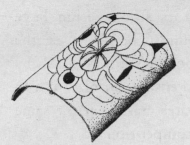

chapter seven

Kee-sup was so busy with the King's kite that he did not have time to fly his own. Young-sup went alone to the hillside nearly every day with his tiger. It was not only for the pleasure of flying. Now he was practicing with a purpose.

The New Year was approaching. It was the biggest holiday of the year. The celebration lasted for fifteen days—gifts were exchanged, grand meals were eaten, visitors came and went. But this year the holiday had gained extra significance for Young-sup.

Every year the holiday culminated in a kite festival. Hundreds, even thousands, of people traveled to the royal park in Seoul to fly kites. And the most important part of the festival was the kite fights.

Young-sup had seen them for the first time the

year before. Two competitors stood within large circles marked on the ground. The object of the contest was to get the opponent's kite to crash by bumping or knocking it. To ensure fair play, and to render a decision if both kites crashed at the same time, judges observed the competition.

The most skillful fliers could sometimes maneuver their kites so that their lines, taut and strong, actually cut through the lines of their opponents. This did not happen often, but when it did, it produced the most exciting victory. As the defeated kite was cut loose and floated off into the sky, dozens of boys chased after it, for the kite now belonged to whoever could reach it first.

Every day, under his tutor's watchful eye, Young-sup struggled to concentrate on his lessons. Normally he prided himself on his studies; indeed, of the two brothers, it was Young-sup who most enjoyed poring over the texts for the challenge of learning the words by heart. But these days all he could think of was the coming festival.

When the lesson finally ended, Young-sup would stand, bow his head, and wait. Sometimes the tutor spent a few moments tidying the scrolls or preparing for the next day's lesson. Young-sup looked like the picture of the dutiful scholar, but every muscle was tense with impatience and inside his head he was screaming, "Hurry up! Forget about all that! Leave!"

When the tutor had stepped through the door, Young-sup was finally free. He walked politely for a few steps, until he saw that the tutor had made the turn for the outer court. Then Young-sup rocketed to his room, grabbed his tiger kite, and raced out to the hillside.

He had but one goal: To be the winner of the boys' competition this year.

....

Young-sup's tiger floated far, far overhead, using nearly all of the line on his reel. He relaxed and let the kite fly almost on its own; practicing was hard work, and he needed a rest. He was alone on the hillside again; Kee-sup was at home studying, trying to catch up on all the lessons he had missed while making the King's kite.

Idly, Young-sup glanced at the landscape. Far down the road that wound around the base of the hill he could see a dark blot approaching. It was too big to be just one person; it must be a group of people. As they slowly drew nearer, Young-sup could make out more details.

Scarlet uniforms. A palanquin. The royal standard atop the palanquin.

The King!

At least this time I'll be ready, thought Young-sup. He began to reel in the line, wishing that Kee-sup were with him.

By the time the King's procession had advanced up the hillside, both the kite and Young-sup were down, the kite with its line wound neatly on the reel and Young-sup on his knees with his forehead touching the ground.

The King dismounted from the palanquin. "Rise," he said. "Where is my kite?"

Young-sup rose to his feet. His mind worked furiously to find the right words. The King's kite was nearly finished; Kee-sup had only the smallest of details to attend to. "Your Majesty, my brother begs your forgiveness. He knows you are waiting, but he—he wishes to make sure the kite is perfect in every way for you."

The King nodded. He turned to his courtiers and gestured with one hand. "All of you are to take the palanquin and wait at the bottom of the hill."

"Your Majesty does not wish any of us to remain?" The man who seemed to be the adviser spoke.

"No. I have no need of assistance. I am merely going to fly a kite." The King seemed impatient.

Young-sup left his kite on the ground and began to follow the others. "Not you," said the King. "You stay."

The guards, servants, and adviser marched down the hill with the empty palanquin. Then the King turned to Young-sup. "I am thinking that I should practice before I fly my new kite."

"Your Majesty is very wise." Young-sup hesitated. "If there is any way I can be of assistance . . ."

The King glanced down the hill at his coterie, then back at Young-sup. "Yes. There is one thing, to begin with. I recall you and your brother last time. You were calling out, shouting to each other. In my travels through the city streets I have heard other boys talk like this."

He paused for a moment. Young-sup thought that the King looked almost embarrassed—then chided himself for having such a thought. Why would the King feel ashamed in front of a lowly subject like himself?

The King continued, "I wish to learn this kind of speech. It cannot be done in the presence of others. But here, on this hillside, I wish for us to speak to each other as you did to your brother."

Young-sup was horrified. Talk to the King like a *brother?* He mumbled, "I could try. If that is what Your Majesty desires."

The King spoke with what sounded almost like a

sigh. "It is what I desire, but perhaps it is not possible. For either of us."

An awkward silence fell between the two boys. Young-sup felt fidgety but forced himself to remain still. He looked down the hill at the King's attendants and wondered what it would be like to be a boy giving commands to grown men.

Giving commands . . . Young-sup's face brightened suddenly. He bowed his head to the King. "Your Majesty?"

"Yes?"

"You could make it a command."

"A command?" The King looked puzzled—then broke into a grin. "Ah, I see! It must be done correctly, then. What is your name?"

"My father is Rice Merchant Lee, Your Majesty. My name is Young-sup, and my brother is Kee-sup."

"Lee Young-sup. When we are alone, you are to speak to me as you speak to your brother. I hereby command you!"

And for the first time Young-sup and the King laughed together.

....

The King was a good flying student. While lacking

Young-sup's natural instinct for flying, he still possessed a better understanding of the wind than Kee-sup had at first. His attempts to launch the tiger kite on his own were unsuccessful, but he did very well at keeping the kite in the air once Young-sup helped him get it there. On Young-sup's advice, the King took off his heavy robe to allow him freer movement. All afternoon the two boys took turns flying, until the sun began to dip below the hilltop.

It was not so difficult for Young-sup to teach the King about flying. To teach him about speaking was another matter entirely.

Young-sup began by explaining. "You know the polite form of speaking—how you use different words to speak to someone older or someone in a higher position? For example, when I thank my father for something, I must use formal words—'Father, I appreciate your kindness.' But to our servant Hwang I might say, 'Thanks, Hwang.'"

The King was holding the reel. He looked doubtful and stared up at the kite for a moment. Then his face cleared a bit. "I remember my lessons, when I was about eight years of age. The court ministers were most annoyed. They kept repeating that I no longer had to address anyone as a superior."

Young-sup listened in astonishment. "Not even

your parents?" As soon as the words left his mouth, he regretted them.

The King spoke solemnly. "My father, His Late Majesty, had passed on to the Heavenly Kingdom. When I became King, the ministers said that no one, not even my mother, the Dowager Queen, was considered my superior."

Young-sup tried to imagine such a thing. He couldn't, and shook his head in wonder.

The King went on, "Instead, my tutors explained that I must always consider carefully whatever I say. They told me that every time I speak, I represent the nation.

"I did not think much of it then, when I was young—I had only to learn it, to please them. But now I am aware that I have spoken in only one way for as long as I can remember. Whereas everyone else, it seems, has different ways of speaking. This is what I wish to learn—these differences."

Young-sup thought hard. How could he explain something that came to him as naturally as breathing? He was silent so long that the King finally spoke.

"Perhaps," His Majesty said wistfully, "it is not something that can be learned."

Young-sup scuffed at the hard ground with his heel a few times to loosen the soil, then sat down. The

King sat next to him. Young-sup showed the King how the reel could be planted in the earth; when the wind was just right, as it was today, the kite could fly even without a flier.

They watched the kite for a few moments. Finally Young-sup asked a question. "Do you ever get angry?"

"Of course."

"What do you say when you get angry?"

"I express my displeasure. If I am angry enough."

Young-sup rolled his eyes and groaned inwardly. He had to think of another way. "Your Majesty, am I truly free to do as I wish now? To teach you the way I speak with my brother?"

"Of course. I have ordered you to do so."

"All right. Let's try something different."

Young-sup picked up the reel, handed it to the King, and stood; the King followed his lead. Then, as the King looked up at the kite, Young-sup shoved him off balance and snatched the reel away from him.

The King staggered backward, then tripped and fell. The watchful guards at the bottom of the hill responded immediately. They charged up the hillside to protect and give aid to the King.

The King jumped to his feet. Without taking his eyes from Young-sup's face, he raised his hand and stopped the guards with a single gesture. They waited where they were, halfway up the hill.

"If it was the reel you desired, why did you not ask me?" The King's voice was stern, his face unsmiling. "It was unnecessary to push me. I would have given it to you."

Young-sup ignored the rebuke. "Your Majesty—when I pushed you just now, what were you thinking? Your exact words, as they were in your mind."

The look on the King's face changed from angry to confused. "I was thinking, Why did you do that?"

"Good!" Young-sup exclaimed. "If it were my brother, that is what he would have said. He would have said something like, 'Why did you do that, you leper?'"

"Ah! So he would have said the words in his mind, just as they were?"

"Yes, that's right."

The King frowned, considering. "And this is how you always speak?"

"No. As I said, I must still use the polite form of address to my parents, my tutor—anyone older. But to others my own age or younger, yes. And also with my brother." Young-sup paused for a moment. "Although now that he has been capped, I'm supposed to speak politely to him as well."

The King nodded. He waved the guards back down the hill, then turned to Young-sup and took a deep breath. "All right. I shall try now." He grabbed for the reel. "Give that back to me, you . . . you leper!"

Young-sup laughed. He held the reel away from the King, then dashed away. The King chased after him. The two boys dodged around the hillside, exchanging insults and laughter as they ran.

At last they slowed, then stopped, still panting and laughing. The King sobered somewhat and beckoned his entourage. As they brought his palanquin back up the hill, he turned to Young-sup. "I'll watch for your kite," he said. "When I see it, I'll come out. If I can."

The King's men had drawn within earshot now. The King straightened up and spoke loudly in a regal voice. "Tell your brother I expect him at the palace soon. You are to come with him."

But his eyes were twinkling, and Young-sup had to suppress a giggle. "Yes, Your Majesty. It shall be so."

chapter eight

The two boys and their father walked in silence. Under Kee-sup's arm, wrapped carefully in a linen cloth, the precious kite was making the journey to the palace.

Kee-sup's use of the gold leaf had been daring—and successful. Using a stiff brush and the blunt edge of a knife, he had flicked and spattered the gold leaf over the whole surface of the kite paper. The rain of minuscule gold dots had resulted in a fine sheen that glowed faintly when the light touched it. Once the kite was in the sky, the sun's rays would make it glitter and shine like real dragon scales.

But this had not been tested. The boys had argued about whether or not the kite should be flown before being presented to the King. Young-sup, of course, had been eager to try it out, but Kee-sup had pre-vailed, fearful of damage to the kite.

Now, as they walked toward the palace, there was little to say. Either the King would like the kite or he would not. Nothing they did or said now could change that.

But Young-sup knew that the kite was more than just a gift for the King. In a few years Kee-sup would take the difficult series of examinations required of those who wished to be employed by the royal court. Such coveted positions were awarded based on the examination results; however, it was well known that those in favor at the court were looked on with added grace. If the King were pleased with the kite, it would do nothing to hurt Kee-sup's chances.

Young-sup carried an extra burden of worry as he walked alongside his brother. He had not told Kee-sup about his recent encounters with the King on the hillside.

The King had come out to fly with him several times, and Young-sup always looked forward to their meetings. At first he told himself that he did not wish to worry Kee-sup by talking about the King while the work on the kite was still progressing. But he knew in his heart that he secretly enjoyed his special friendship with the King, a friendship in which Kee-sup had no part.

As they approached the gates, Young-sup comforted himself with the knowledge that there would probably be other people at the court when they arrived and that the King would be speaking to him only as a subject. Perhaps he would not have to explain anything.

The immense gates opened wide, and the crowd of onlookers that always seemed to hover around the palace watched in surprise and envy as the three Lees were permitted entry. They were escorted across the huge outer court by a pair of guards, who stopped before a closed door.

Here the boys' father left them. "This is for you to do," he said, addressing Kee-sup. "I will see you at home." They bowed to him and watched as he crossed the courtyard to the outer gates.

With one of the guards the boys stepped into a small antechamber. The huge carved doors opposite them were opened by two other guards, revealing a grand hall. The boys barely had time for a quick gape at the splendid silk hangings and other priceless works of art before they spied the throne at the far end of the hall. At once they dropped to their knees.

"You may rise and approach." The King's voice seemed to echo down the long empty space.

The brothers got to their feet and walked toward the King. They saw that he was flanked by several advisers and guards.

When they were within a few paces of the throne, Kee-sup unwrapped the kite and laid it flat across his two hands. He held it out before him as he bowed his head.

The King glanced at it without apparent interest. Then he spoke loudly. "Go, all of you. Leave us." The adviser whom Young-sup knew from the hillside seemed to hesitate, but a glare from the King had him hastily retreating after the others.

The King waited until the huge carved doors had closed again. Then he hopped down off the throne and took the kite from Kee-sup's outstretched hands. His face shone with open delight.

"This is wonderful! Better than I could have imagined. Look at how it sparkles!" He tilted the kite to and fro for a few moments, then looked at Kee-sup. "This is even better than the tiger kites!"

Kee-sup stammered as he answered. "I—I am honored that Your Majesty is pleased with the kite."

Young-sup saw the startled look on Kee-sup's face and sensed at once the source of his brother's discomfort. He cleared his throat and addressed the King. "I think you will have to command him, the same as you did with me."

"Oh, that. Yes, of course. Kee-sup, isn't it? Lee Kee-sup, when we are alone, you are not to address me as the King. Just act as if I'm any old—any old—"

"—pig-brain," Young-sup finished for him.

Kee-sup looked for a moment as though he might faint. But the King only laughed and gave Young-sup a shove.

"Who are you calling pig-brain, you cow-dung?"

Young-sup would have continued the banter, but one look at the shocked and confused expression on Kee-sup's face gave him pause.

"Brother, I'm sorry. The King has been coming to the hillside to fly with me. I meant to tell you. . . . I just—I just never found the right moment." He looked at Kee-sup pleadingly. "It's all right, brother. We always make sure no one can hear us, like now. Besides"—and his joking tone returned—"what can I do? The King has commanded me to call him a pig-brain!"

At that Kee-sup laughed and appeared to relax, but Young-sup could see that he was still not entirely at ease.

The King, too, seemed to sense it, and began to

speak more seriously. "I am glad you came, because I've been thinking about something, and I need to talk to you—to both of you," he said. "Come."

He led them through a side door into a smaller room. There they sat on cushions around a low table. The King summoned a servant and ordered tea and sweets to be brought. The three boys ate and drank in silence. Then the King put his cup down.

"I want to talk to you about the New Year kite festival," he said.

....

The New Year holiday was in the next moon, and like the brothers themselves, the King was most excited about the kite festival. He was personally planning the events of the final day.

"I was thinking about competing in the festival myself," the King explained.

Young-sup felt a wave of panic. Would he have to fly against the King?

But the King was still speaking. "I decided not to, for a couple of reasons. First, I don't think I'm good enough yet. I can't launch by myself every time. And I need a lot more practice with fighting maneuvers. But that's not really the most important reason." He paused, his face sober. "If I fly in the competition, I don't think anyone will try to beat me. I'm the King—so everyone will just let me win. It wouldn't be a real competition. Don't you agree?"

The brothers nodded; Young-sup had been thinking that very thing.

The King sighed. "But I still want to be part of it, somehow. I thought that even if *I* don't compete, perhaps my kite can." He looked at his companions expectantly. "Kee-sup, you have made the kite—a kite truly worthy of a King. It deserves to be in the competition."

Kee-sup bowed his head in appreciation.

"As for you, Young-sup—I want you to fly it for me. But I don't want anyone to know that you're my flier. If people find out, it would be the same as if I were flying it myself—no one would try to beat you."

Young-sup felt his heartbeat quicken. Blood rushed to his face, and he could sense that he must be as red as a peony blossom. He was dazzled by the thought. To fly for the King! It was an honor beyond imagining.

Through the haze of surprise, he heard Kee-sup's voice. "I speak for both my brother and myself when

I say that this could be kept a secret from all except our father. We could not keep such an honor and responsibility from him."

"Of course," the King answered at once. His voice grew thoughtful. "It is good that you feel such a duty to your father." Something about the way he said this reminded the other two that the King himself had no father, and for a moment the room was filled with a heavy silence.

"Well, then," the King said briskly. "It's agreed. Enough talk—let's go outside."

And he led the way through the palace, through room after vast room filled with wondrous treasures—jade carvings, ivory statues, enormous chests inlaid with mother-of-pearl. They saw no other people, except an occasional shadowy servant or a guard standing motionless by a door.

At last they reached the royal gardens. The King pulled something from his pocket and tossed it into the air, and the three boys at once began a rousing game of kick-the-shuttlecock.

The "cock" was a coin, wrapped around and about its central hole with strips of paper. The ends of these strips formed tassels that fluttered gaily and made a pleasant sound as the cock was kicked by the side of the foot. The object was to try to keep the cock off the ground as long as possible without using one's hands.

The King proved to be a wizard at the game. He juggled the cock inside his foot, outside, on his knee, and back again, ten, twenty, thirty times without missing. After they had kicked the cock among them for a while, the King gave a solo demonstration. Kee-sup counted out loud for the King while Young-sup clowned around, trying to distract him. The rest of the afternoon passed without any thought or talk of kites or kingship. The brothers departed from the palace with a promise to come again soon.

On the way home Young-sup couldn't stop himself from enthusing over the splendor of the palace and the fun they had had. He did not speak of the honor that had been bestowed on him, although the thought never left his mind and seemed to float beneath his every word.

Soon, however, he noticed his brother's quietness.

"What is it, brother? Didn't you have a good time? Aren't you glad that the King was so pleased with the kite?"

Kee-sup nodded absently. "I wasn't thinking about

all that. I was thinking about how good he was at kicking the cock." He stopped walking and turned his head to look at the imposing wall of the palace in the distance behind them. Then he turned back and walked on, speaking almost to himself. "Shuttlecock . . . a game you can play when you have no one to play with."

chapter nine

The brothers reached home just before dinner. As usual their mother served her husband and sons first; she and the girls would eat later. And as usual the meal was eaten in silence. It was considered good manners to give one's full attention to the food. So it was not until after eating that the boys had a chance to speak to their father.

They sat side by side on the floor in their father's room. Kee-sup told him how pleased the King had been with the kite and that they had drunk tea with him. Then he told of the King's plan for the New Year kite competition. He did not mention their growing friendship with the King; instinctively, both boys felt their father would have disapproved. He would have said that the King was their ruler, not their friend.

When Kee-sup finished speaking, their father folded his arms and looked over their heads, staring at nothing. The boys waited.

At last he spoke, addressing Young-sup. "You are to fly the kite. Was this commanded by the King?"

Young-sup hesitated. "I—I'm not sure, Father. No, it was not exactly a command. More like a request."

His father nodded. "His Majesty knows well the teachings of the master Confucius. In his youthful enthusiasm he may have forgotten."

His voice held a tone Young-sup had heard many times before. He squeezed his eyes shut for a moment, as if to quell the rising dread in his heart.

"Always the eldest son represents the family. When you next see the King, ask him if he would be so good as to grant my wish for Kee-sup to fly the kite at the festival." And he nodded toward the door to dismiss them.

....

The brothers did not look at each other as they walked toward their room. Kee-sup slid open the paper door and stepped inside. Young-sup closed the door behind them.

His face felt like a stone. Bitterness rose through

him until he could taste it in his mouth. He could not rage as he wished, for the paper walls were thin, but he spoke in a low voice forced out between his set jaws.

"Always you."

Kee-sup took a deep breath, but Young-sup was still speaking. "*You* get to go to the mountains. *You* get a kite for New Year. *You* fly the kite at the festival. You—you—you!"

"Brother, I—"

"Nothing else matters! Second son—what's that? I might as well be a dog! I don't matter to him—he doesn't care anything about me." Young-sup took care not to raise his voice, but his rage was bubbling over now.

"That's not true! He bought the seventh kite for you—" Too late Kee-sup cut off his words.

Young-sup's fury was interrupted in mid-flow. "The seventh kite? You mean, that day at the market? The day I won the reel?" He could hear his own voice, pitched high in shock and confusion. "No, he couldn't have. I remember—it was a little boy who bought the last kite. I saw him myself."

"The money," Kee-sup explained, misery in his face. "It was our father who gave the boy the money for the kite."

Young-sup blinked and shook his head quickly, as if waking. Then he looked squarely at his brother. "Because *you* asked him to." There was no answer. "I'm right, aren't I? He didn't do it for me—he did it because it was what *you* wanted."

Young-sup clenched his fists and stiffened his body, as if the anger in him were a pain he could no longer bear. Then he swung around and seized the first thing that caught his eye—the ceramic jar that had once held the gold leaf. He hurled it to the floor with all his strength and fled from the room.

....

The next morning the boys did not speak to each other. They studied their lessons side by side, as they always did, but even their tutor noticed the tension between them. Young-sup's responses were dull and mechanical, and Kee-sup's so absent-minded that the tutor scolded them both.

For Young-sup, learning the teachings of Confucius and the events of Korean history was not as important as it was for his brother. Young-sup knew he was expected to take over his father's business as a rice merchant. Merchants did not have as much need of education as courtiers. Still, Young-sup studied at his father's insistence, to keep Kee-sup company and help him whenever possible.

Young-sup usually enjoyed the challenge of learning by heart the words on the scrolls. Today, though, he felt drained of all interest, and it seemed that Kee-sup felt the same way. Finally the tutor spoke sternly. "There is no desire for learning in either of you," he announced. "You are both to study this lesson again and be ready to recite it to me tomorrow."

The tutor left the room, and the boys sat for a few moments in an uncomfortable silence. Then Young-sup spoke. His jaw felt sore, as if his teeth had been clenched from the moment he had learned that he would not fly for the King. "You go first," he said woodenly. He picked up the scroll from its place on the table between them and held it so that Kee-sup could not see the words.

The lesson, the Five Virtues of Confucius, was familiar to both boys, but the examinations required perfect memorization of every word. Kee-sup began to recite:

"Between father and son: love from the father, duty from the son.

"Between king and subjects: fairness from the king, loyalty from his subjects.

"Between husband and wife: kindness from the husband, obedience from the wife.

"Between older and younger: consideration from the older, respect from the younger.

"Between friend and friend: faith from each to the other."

He stumbled over only a few words, Young-sup prompting him. Then Young-sup held out the scroll and prepared for his turn to recite.

Kee-sup didn't move to take the scroll. He was staring at the tabletop, his brow furrowed in ferocious concentration, the deepest of frowns on his face. Young-sup glanced down to see what held his interest; there was nothing there.

"Here," he said impatiently, and shook the scroll so it rattled a little. "What are you looking at?"

Kee-sup looked up suddenly and waved the words away as if they were bothersome gnats. "Hush. I was thinking about something . . ." He jumped to his feet. "We'll study later. There's something I have to do." And with Young-sup still holding the scroll in puzzled surprise, Kee-sup left the room.

....

Later that afternoon Young-sup wandered into the kitchen. He watched listlessly as his mother and the maidservant taught his little sisters how to make *man-doo*, meat-stuffed dumplings. After a quick glance at Young-sup's sullen face, they ignored him. His mother knew that if he wanted to speak, he would.

Not being allowed to fly the kite for the King—that was the biggest disappointment. Young-sup considered for a moment the possibility of flying his own tiger kite in the competition. He discarded the idea just as quickly. If he should end up flying against Kee-sup, he knew in his heart that he could win. And he also knew that he wouldn't even try. Just as the King had said, a contest with a fixed result was not worth competing in.

But on top of that his great joy in earning the reel had been crushed. He hadn't really won it on his own, after all. The knowledge bit into him like the sting of a centipede, and he felt he would never again use the reel with pleasure.

He stared at the low tabletop, where the hands of the two women were nearly a blur as they flashed about filling and sealing the dumplings. His sisters made awkward, lumpy dumplings; perhaps if he hung around long enough, he could snitch a few of these straight from the pot. It seemed the only thing in life to look forward to now.

It was there that Kee-sup found him, crouched glumly by the low iron stove as the simmering dumplings filled the tiny room with their aromatic steam.

"Come on," said Kee-sup. "Let's go to the hillside and fly."

Young-sup scowled. "You go. You're the one who needs the practice."

Kee-sup's voice was stubborn. "You come, too." He stepped a little closer and lowered his voice. "We need to talk."

Young-sup sighed and rose to his feet. Kee-sup had left both tiger kites outside the kitchen doorhole, and each carried his own on the long walk up the hill.

As always flying had the power to cheer Young-sup. He never tired of the thrill that ran through him when he felt the tug of the wind on his line. And it surprised him to find that holding his reel again was a great comfort. It was still his reel, fine and shining, no matter who had paid for the seventh kite. The pain eased as he flew, like a swelling going down.

So he was ready to listen when his brother began to

speak. Kee-sup's words came slowly, with a night and a day of thought behind them.

"You think it's so easy for me, being the first-born," he began. "Well, you're wrong. I could tell you hundreds of times when I wished things were different."

Young-sup turned in surprise. He had imagined the talk would be about kite-fighting strategy, and no matter how deep his own disappointment he had concluded that not to help Kee-sup would serve no purpose. He had come to the hillside prepared to give his brother a flying lesson.

Kee-sup went on. "Do you think I always *want* to go to the ancestors' gravesite? Four times a year, the same thing over and over. It was fun at first. Now it's just something I have to do. There are lots of times I'd rather stay home.

"And what about our studies? You know I will take the court examinations in a few years. Study, study, study—that's all Father ever talks about. Remember during the spring rains when we both caught colds? You stayed in bed for days. Not me— I had to keep studying. Father said I couldn't afford to lose the time."

As his brother spoke, Young-sup realized what he had known all along—that he wasn't really angry at

Kee-sup. But he dared not be angry at his father, either; it was forbidden by the tradition of filial duty. Whom was he angry at, then?

"Do you want to know the worst thing? No one has ever asked me if I *want* to be a scholar. I don't. I want to do something with my hands. But that kind of work doesn't get you a position at the court. So I spend all my time working at something I don't even want to do."

Kee-sup stopped talking long enough to bring his kite down. He looked back up at Young-sup's kite and spoke while staring skyward. "Well, today I finally did something I wanted. I spoke to our father and asked him to allow you to fly the King's kite in the competition."

Young-sup was so startled that for a few moments he paid no attention to his kite; it took a great swooping dive and seemed as surprised as he was. Quickly he controlled it again, then asked, "What did he say?"

"What do you think?" Kee-sup's eyes began to twinkle a little. "You ought to know—you're the one who said he always does what I ask."

Young-sup shook his head in disbelief. "How did you convince him?"

"I told him that only the best flier should represent

our family honor—and that you were the best. I asked him to come to the hillside to see for himself, if he wanted."

"How did you dare—" Young-sup's voice was almost a whisper.

Kee-sup shrugged. "It was our lesson this morning, the Five Virtues. I have a duty to our father, it's true. But I have other duties as well. To the King, as his subject. To you, as your elder brother. And to both of you, as friends."

Kee-sup grinned. "I counted. It was four duties against one."

Young-sup was too big to cry, but a lump of joy formed in his throat. He could not look at his brother, knowing well that Kee-sup was making light of what must have been a terrible encounter. To confront their father about a decision he had already made was a taboo of the greatest order, and Young-sup did not even want to guess what the conversation had been like.

Kee-sup shoved him good-naturedly. "Come on, little brother. We have work to do if you're going to win for the King."

chapter ten

*I*f Young-sup had wanted to win the competition before, it was nothing compared to how he felt now. Now he was flying for the King and for himself. But most of all he was flying for his brother—to prove to their father that Kee-sup had been right about who should fly.

The days leading to the New Year were for Young-sup like the motions of a dragonfly's wings—repeated flying sessions that blurred into a single endless practice. He still had to attend to his studies and do all the usual everyday things. But most of his waking hours were spent with the kite, either on the hillside or in his mind.

One night Young-sup awoke with a cry. He was flailing around on his sleeping mat, his arms and hands making desperate movements, as if trying to control a kite line. Kee-sup was kneeling beside the mat, shaking his shoulder.

"Hush, brother, it's all right. You were only dreaming."

"He was cutting my line!" Young-sup spoke frantically. "I couldn't stop him. The King's kite—I was about to lose the King's kite . . ." Not until Kee-sup lit the lantern was Young-sup able to banish the dream demon and come to himself at last.

Of the myriad skills involved in kite fighting, it was the line cutting that most worried him. To help him practice this difficult skill, Kee-sup had hastily made a dozen simple kites. He would fly one while Young-sup practiced the careful positioning and the manipulation of the reel that enabled his line to saw through an opponent's. When he was successful, Kee-sup's kite would fly off into the distance. Sometimes one fell close enough to retrieve, but the boys did not have time to chase those that flew far away. So Kee-sup made sure always to have another kite on hand.

During practice that day Young-sup had twice been able to cut the line of Kee-sup's kite. But after the second time he reeled in, shaking his head.

"What's the matter?" Kee-sup demanded. "That last cut was pretty good."

"The problem is that your kite just sits there, waiting for me to make the right move. That's not what's going to happen at the competition. They'll be trying to cut my line as hard as I'm trying to cut theirs."

"I haven't been just sitting there," Kee-sup protested. "I'm doing my best to try to dodge you."

"I know, I know," Young-sup replied hastily. "I didn't mean—I mean, this practice has been really helpful. But I wish I had some way of being certain that I will be the first to cut the line."

....

After a day of study and practice both boys were exhausted. They could barely keep their eyes open as they rolled out their sleeping mats. That evening Young-sup was feeling especially sluggish. As he spread his blankets out, he felt a sharp prick on his hand.

"*Ai!*" he gasped, and examined his hand at once. It was bleeding from the tiniest of cuts.

"What happened?"

"I don't know. I was just spreading my blankets on the floor when something cut me. It's fine now—it's not even bleeding anymore."

"Yes, but what was it? You'd better find it so neither of us gets cut again."

The boys moved Young-sup's mat and blankets to one side and carefully inspected the tile floor. They saw nothing, so Kee-sup fetched the lantern that hung by the door and held it down low.

Here and there a nearly invisible point caught the light and shone.

Young-sup cautiously touched his fingertip to one such point and looked at it closely.

"What is it?"

"I think it might be a tiny bit of pottery or something," said Young-sup. "Oh, I know." He looked up sheepishly. "That day I threw the jar—remember? You swept it up for me, but you must have missed these tiny pieces. I'll fetch a damp cloth—the broom would probably just miss them again."

Once the floor had been wiped and dried, the boys crawled wearily into bed. Just as Young-sup was dropping off to sleep, he heard Kee-sup's voice.

"Brother?"

"What?"

"That tiny piece of pottery. It actually cut you?"

"Yes—so what? I want to go to sleep."

Kee-sup sounded half-asleep himself as he answered. "Just an idea I have. I'll tell you . . . some other time . . ."

....

When Young-sup awoke, his brother's sleeping mat was still on the floor, but there was no sign of Kee-sup anywhere. Young-sup got up, folded their blankets, and rolled up both mats. As he was putting them away in the low cupboard, the door slid open and Kee-sup stepped inside. He was carrying something.

"Where have you been? And why aren't you wearing your good clothes?" It was the first day of the New Year celebration, and they were to be dressed in their best.

"I forgot," Kee-sup confessed. He put some pieces of broken pottery down on the cupboard and began to change.

"What are those for?" Young-sup nodded at the odd bits of pottery. Some were from the jar he had thrown, others he didn't recognize, perhaps from a pot or bowl that had been broken in the kitchen.

"Just wait. I'll show you later." And for the moment Kee-sup would say nothing more.

....

That morning, as the brothers and their father were finishing breakfast, they heard pounding at the gate. Hwang rushed to open it. The boys' uncle and his family had arrived from the city of Inchon, which lay to the west on the Yellow Sea.

It was the only time of year when the two families were united, for the road from Inchon, where their father's brother worked as a fisherman, was long and difficult. Uncle's family was large: three boys and three girls, all younger than Young-sup. The littlest was only a baby, and some of the younger ones were shy and bewildered, clinging closely to their mother.

The visitors would be staying for nearly the whole holiday. The house filled with noise and activity as the adults bustled about putting away bags and parcels. Then the cousins changed into their holiday clothes. Everyone met in the Hall of Ancestors for the bowing ceremony.

The adults sat at one end of the room on cushions. One by one, each child came forward and bowed low, all the way down to the ground. Upon rising, he or she received a gift of money from each adult, with the child's age determining how much was given.

Kee-sup, as the eldest son of the eldest son, began the ceremony. Each child took a turn, and with his mother's help even the baby bowed, causing great shouts of laughter from everyone.

After the bowing ceremony ended, the games began. Children and adults alike played the board game *yut,* and *hwa-toe,* a card game. And throughout the day everyone collected "nines."

Kee-sup had written the Chinese character for "long life" on a large piece of paper. He showed it to everyone and explained it to the younger cousins.

"You see this symbol? It means 'long life' in Chinese. This"— he pointed to part of the symbol— "means 'life.' And these two parts at the beginning are 'nines.' That's why nine is lucky. The more nines you collect today, the luckier your year will be."

The collecting of nines began.

"I've picked up nine stones."

"I counted nine birds in the sky."

"I kicked the shuttlecock nine times without missing."

Even the adults participated, with the boys' mother presenting a tray of nine different kinds of cakes, and their father giving each child a bag of nine nuts. And their aunt got the biggest laugh of all when she announced that she would change the baby's diaper nine times that day.

chapter eleven

The games and feasting would continue for fifteen days. But on that first day, as Young-sup was kicking the shuttlecock with his cousins, Kee-sup beckoned him, and they slipped away from the game playing.

Kee-sup sent him to the kitchen for a bowl of left-over cooked rice. "Then find Hwang and ask him for a wooden mallet."

"A mallet, brother? What for?"

"Just go," said Kee-sup impatiently. "Meet me back in our room."

When Young-sup arrived, out of breath and with mallet and bowl in hand, he found Kee-sup wrapping the pieces of broken pottery in a cloth.

"Now tell me," Young-sup demanded.

Kee-sup shook his head. "It will be easier to show

you." He tied the corners of the cloth securely, put the bundle on a piece of paper on the floor, and took up the mallet. Then he smashed the bundle as hard as he could.

There was a sound of breaking porcelain, muffled by the cloth. Kee-sup hit the cloth again and again. From time to time, he poked gingerly at the bundle. It took a long time and many blows of the mallet, but at last the pieces of pottery had been broken and ground almost to a powder.

Kee-sup untied the cloth and left it on the floor. He cut a length of line from his reel, then took a few grains of rice from the bowl. With the rice on his fingertips, he rubbed and rolled the line repeatedly until it was coated with stickiness.

"The broken stuff—spread it out on the paper," he ordered. Young-sup complied, using a spoon to scoop up and spread the ground pottery.

Kee-sup held the line taut between his hands and rolled it in the powdered pottery until the center section of the line was well coated. He inspected it critically, rolled it again, and hung it up to dry. Young-sup watched all this in silence.

Kee-sup tidied up the work area a little, then spoke. "When you cut your hand last night, it gave me an idea. If a single tiny piece of broken pottery could cut your hand, maybe a lot of them together could cut through a kite line."

Young-sup's eyes widened in surprise and admiration. "That's a great idea—if it works."

The boys each checked the line a dozen times that day. It wasn't until the evening that the heavy mixture of rice paste and powdered pottery was completely dry.

Kee-sup held the coated piece of line and pulled it taut. Facing him, Young-sup held a plain piece of line. They crossed the two pieces and rubbed them against each other.

Young-sup's line began to fray almost immediately. After just a few sawing motions, his piece was cut through.

....

It was a triumphant pair that walked back from the hillside the next afternoon. Together they had coated an arm's length of Young-sup's line nearest the kite with the pottery-and-glue mixture and had let it dry overnight. They found that the cutting edge worked just as well in the air as it had in their room; Young-sup cut the lines of three kites in a row with no trouble.

As they were busy congratulating each other, Young-sup had a sudden, sobering thought.

"Brother. What if it's against the rules?"

"Against the rules?" Kee-sup stopped in his tracks. "I never thought of that. You mean, maybe someone has thought of this before and it's not allowed."

"We could ask."

"But if we ask another flier, and no one *has* thought of it before, maybe he'll steal our idea."

They stared at each other, their faces reflections of worry.

All at once Young-sup thrust his kite at his brother. "Here—take my kite. I'll see you at home in a little while."

He turned and ran off down the road.

"Where are you going?" Kee-sup called.

Young-sup turned back for a moment. "I've thought of someone I can ask."

....

"Honorable sir!"

Kite Seller Chung lifted his head. He was just leaving the marketplace after a busy day.

Young-sup rushed up to him, panting from his run, and bowed politely if hurriedly. The old kite seller smiled at his eagerness.

"What demon chases you, young flier?" he teased.

"No demon, sir—just a question."

"A question for me, I take it."

Young-sup looked around them. The market was closing for the day, with many people brushing past them in their hurry to make last-minute purchases. He bowed again to the old man.

"I do not wish to delay you, sir. Perhaps we could talk as I walk beside you."

The old man cocked his head curiously and gestured his assent. They set out on the road away from the market and walked in silence until the crowds around them had thinned somewhat.

"Now, young flier. What is this question, the answer to which you believe I hold?"

"It's about the kite festival, sir. About the competition."

"Ah—the kite fights." The old man's eyes lit up with keen interest.

"Yes, sir. It is said that there is little you do not know about them."

The kite seller nodded. "True enough. I have been watching them every year now for more than half a hundred years."

"Then you would know, sir, about the rules." Young-sup paused, his voice low and urgent. "My brother has a new . . . invention. We wish to use it at the fights, but we need to know if using it would be honorable—within the rules."

His companion frowned. "That is not one question, young flier, but two. Tell me about this invention."

Young-sup described what his brother had done and how it worked. The old man stroked his chin thoughtfully as he listened, but when Young-sup described how easily the pottery-coated line had cut the lines of three kites in a row, he let out a single shout of laughter.

"Ha! He is a clever boy, your brother. I remember him now. He used to come by my stall often enough last year, to ask questions about kite making. But I have not seen him for many months."

They walked on in silence, Young-sup fidgeting anxiously at the man's side. At last the kite seller asked a question.

"Could anyone—a flier without skill, for instance—cut down a kite with this special line?"

Young-sup shook his head. "No, sir. The kite must be controlled correctly, and the motions to cut the line must be precise. It's just quicker, that's all."

The man stopped walking and faced the boy.

"Then here are my answers. Is this invention within the rules? Yes. There is nothing that forbids it."

Young-sup drew a quick breath. The kite seller raised his hand as a caution.

"But there is a more difficult question. From what you have told me, it is clearly a great advantage—perhaps too great. Yet you say that there would be no advantage without skill. It is you yourself, and your brother, who must decide if it is honorable."

Young-sup bowed in farewell and thanks. The old man returned his bow.

"I will be watching for you at the competition, young flier. The best of luck to you, whatever you decide."

chapter twelve

The King dismissed his courtiers, then bounded down from the throne.

"I'm so glad you came! I've been seeing your kites from the garden. I wanted to come out, but I couldn't. It's been so busy here because of the holiday."

It was three days before the competition. Kee-sup and Young-sup had come to the palace on two missions: To fetch the King's kite for a few practice sessions and to discuss the use of the special line.

They sat again in the small room off the throne hall. A servant brought a tray of sweets, the fanciest and most delicious the two brothers had ever eaten. There were cakes with honey and almonds, with pine nuts, with hidden pockets of sweet bean paste. It was hard not to be greedy.

"Good, aren't they?" said the King when they had finished. "Special, for the New Year. Now, it looks as though you have something to tell me. And I have something to tell you. Who shall go first?"

"You, of course, *Your Majesty*," Young-sup mocked.

"Very funny. Well, I will, anyway. I have two things to tell you. First, I was thinking about last year's kite fights. I remembered that everyone was talking about the boy who won, because he had also won the year before."

The King wrinkled his brow in thought. "His name is Kim Hee-nam. He will be your greatest competition. I don't think anyone else from last year can fly like you"—he looked at Young-sup—"and certainly no one else will have so fine a kite." Kee-sup nodded a tiny bow of thanks at the compliment.

"The second thing. I know I made the right decision not to fly myself. But Kee-sup, you made the kite, and Young-sup, you will fly it. What am *I* doing? Nothing. I want to do *something*—even something little. So I've been thinking and thinking, and finally an idea came to me."

The King rose from his cushion and crossed the room. On a shelf stood a lacquerware box. He lifted the lid, took something out, and brought it back to the table.

It was a large hank of sky-blue silk line. The brothers touched it curiously.

"It's the finest-quality line. I didn't get a reel, because I thought you would want to use yours." He nodded at Young-sup.

"Why blue?" Kee-sup asked.

The King's eyes shone. "That's the best part. I thought that a line this color would be harder to see, you know, with the sky behind it. If your opponents can't see the line very well, they may have more difficulty cutting it."

Young-sup shouted with laughter. "An invisible line! What an idea!" And Kee-sup, too, was enthusiastic.

The King was pleased. "Now, what did you want to tell me?"

The brothers grew sober at once. Kee-sup explained in detail the process of making the pottery-coated line. Young-sup spoke of using it, and of his conversation with the old kite seller. He finished by saying, "We are flying for you, so we thought you should be the one to decide."

The King folded his arms and furrowed his brow. He stared at nothing for a long moment while the brothers waited.

"It's like this." The King spoke thoughtfully. "The

best way to win is with a line cut, right? Not only because it's the most exciting, but also because its form is the finest. You don't have one kite crashing to the ground. Instead, the losing kite flies away. That's a much more dignified way for a kite and a flier to lose, don't you think?"

Young-sup felt a quiet admiration for the King on hearing his words. He glanced at Kee-sup and sensed from his expression that his brother felt the same.

The King continued, "I am thinking that this year using the line could indeed be a great advantage. But not next year. Next year everyone will be doing it." He grinned. "Can you imagine next year's competition? How exciting it will be!"

So it was decided. Young-sup would fly the King's dragon kite, made by Kee-sup, on a pottery-coated sky-blue line.

chapter thirteen

It was the last day of the New Year celebration—the day of the kite festival. Kee-sup and Young-sup walked the road to the royal park together. Their uncle's family had departed the day before, and their father had sent word from his room that he would join them later.

Since the day of the confrontation with Kee-sup, their father had not spoken of the kite festival. Both boys knew that it was not because of his normal reserve. Behind his silence lay great disapproval.

But the brothers were determined not to think about that now. Kee-sup carried the King's kite, attached with the sky-blue line to Young-sup's reel. The day before, the line had been carefully prepared. Part of it had been coated with the special mixture of rice-paste glue and powdered pottery. Then Kee-sup had tied the line, using the usual four-leg bridle, so that the coated section was attached near the kite itself.

Young-sup carried two small "wishing" kites, his own and Kee-sup's. The wishing kites would be used as part of the kite festival.

What crowds there were as the boys approached the park! Gaily decorated stalls along the road sold food, drink, kites, and toys. Everyone was in high spirits; friends called out to one another and boasted of their kites and their flying skills.

Fearful for the King's kite, Kee-sup sometimes had to raise it straight over his head to keep it from being damaged in the crush. At last they reached the great open space in the center of the park where the festival would be held.

As they walked about in search of a place to sit down and rest, Young-sup realized his brother had just spoken to him. He looked up, embarrassed. "Sorry, brother, I didn't hear you. I've been counting my steps—by nines."

Kee-sup grinned. "I've been counting every nine people we pass." The brothers laughed, no longer alone in their anxiety.

In the center of the open space two large circles

had already been marked on the ground. At the far end of the field a long, low platform had been built, and a silk tent erected on it. This was the temporary throne room from which the King would observe the day's festivities.

For the moment the throne stood empty, but as the brothers drank tea and rested from their long walk, a soldier mounted the platform and struck a mighty blow on the brass gong that stood at one end.

Immediately the crowd of thousands stopped whatever they were doing—talking, eating, drinking, flying—and dropped to their knees. After a second gong a splendid procession entered the park: a host of scarlet-clad soldiers, followed by the royal palanquin and then many more soldiers. Once the palanquin had passed by, a subject was allowed to rise to his feet, so a great wave of movement rippled through the crowd as the people rose, several dozen at a time.

The King mounted the platform to address the crowd. As usual at such large gatherings, there were soldiers stationed throughout the park to serve as "shouters." The first of them stood quite near the platform, where he could hear the King easily. He would call out, repeating the King's words to the crowd surrounding him and to the next shouter, who was standing farther away. Each shouter would repeat the King's words until even the far reaches of the crowd had heard them.

"My people! I greet you on this fifteenth day of the New Year. May our ancestors bless our land and our people in the year to come, with good fortune for all!"

As the King paused to let the shouters do their work, his words echoed through the great park. Young-sup looked around at all the solemn, attentive faces and felt a secret pleasure at the thought of having the King as a friend,

"He sounds very 'royal,' doesn't he?" Kee-sup whispered. Young-sup grinned, knowing his brother shared the same thoughts.

The King was speaking again. "It is my first official act of this New Year to open the kite festival. I honor our traditions by performing this duty with the release of the first wishing kite."

A stirring of surprise rolled through the crowd as the King's words spread, for it had been expected that, as in years past, the wishing kites would *close* the festival, not open it.

But the King paid no heed to the murmurs in the crowd. One of his courtiers handed him a small kite and reel. Tied to the line was a bit of oil-soaked rag.

The King stepped to the edge of the platform and waited as the courtier lit a fire-stick from a lantern and touched the rag with the stick, setting it aflame. The courtier then helped the King launch the kite.

As the kite rose, the flame burned through the rag. The crowd watched in silence until the rag had burned enough for the flame to reach the line. Then the line itself burned through, releasing the kite.

The enormous roar that rose from the crowd seemed to push the freed kite higher and higher into the skies. Like all the other wishing kites, the King's kite had been painted with the Chinese characters "Bad luck—go!" Tradition had it that the kite would carry away a whole year of misfortune.

Then the King raised his arms and nodded at the crowd, which burst into activity as people prepared to launch their own wishing kites. Some kites had bits of rag or sulfur-paper tied to their lines. The brothers' wishing kites were attached to short lengths of line rather than a full reel and would be released when all the line had been let out.

At a signal from the King, a guard hit the gong, and the wishing kites were launched. More than a thousand of them rose into the air, at first jostling and bumping one another like the people in the crowd below, then finding more space and sky as they were released.

Disease. Hunger. Unhappiness. As the kites flew off like a huge flock of strange white birds, it seemed truly possible that all the unlucky things in life were being carried away.

....

Now the King declared the start of the kite-fighting competition. Boys fifteen years of age or younger would compete first, followed by the men. For a time there was great confusion. Soldiers cleared the competition field and formed a line around the edge of it to keep the spectators back. Competitors were told to line up on one side of the field. Three judges joined the King on the platform to observe the fights.

Young-sup's eyes met his brother's for a brief moment, then Kee-sup looked down and touched the kite's red-and-gold scales one last time. "Fly well, brother."

Young-sup nodded but could not speak. He took the dragon from Kee-sup and began making his way through the crowd to the fighters' line.

The competition would be run knock-out style. The fliers would fight two at a time; the loser would be eliminated, and the winner would get back in line to await the next round. Each round would see the elimination of half the fighters, until only two were left. These two competitors would fight for the championship.

Although thousands of men and boys had come to the park that day, most of them would not fight. Only a few dozen boys believed they possessed the necessary skill to fight before the King himself. No boy or man would have considered fighting unless he were truly expert; to display oneself poorly at such a gathering would bring great dishonor to one's whole family.

Young-sup found himself in the middle of the line. He looked quickly at the boys and their kites. Not one of them held a finer kite than the red dragon; indeed, it had already drawn many admiring glances.

The boy ahead of him nodded a greeting. "See that fellow down there, the tall one?" He indicated a boy a full head taller than Young-sup himself standing near the end of the line. "That's Kim Hee-nam, the champion. He has won the competition two years in a row. No one else has ever done that. I hope I don't have to fly against him."

Immediately, Young-sup's interest sharpened. He studied the champion closely. The tall boy's face was calm and emotionless, unlike the anxious expressions of most of those in the line. His kite was plain cream-colored paper, and he held it almost casually. Everything about him indicated confidence in his own abilities.

Kim Hee-nam, thought Young-sup, *I hope I do fly against you.*

....

In the first several fights none of the competitors attempted a line cut. A fighter was eliminated in one of two ways. Either he lost control of his kite because of bumping or knocking by the opponent, and the kite dove to the ground; or, in his attempts to maneuver, he stepped out of the white chalk circle. Most of the fights were several minutes long, although a particularly hard-fought battle might last a quarter of an hour or more.

Posted near each circle was a soldier whose sole responsibility was to watch the feet of the fighters. The soldier held a bamboo stick with a red silk square tied to one end, which he raised high in the air if a fighter stepped outside the circle. Young-sup felt a little sorry for these soldiers, who were never able to look up and watch the excitement of the fights.

At last Young-sup reached the head of the line. The

boy behind him, against whom he would fight, looked to be about his age and size; Young-sup had glanced at him surreptitiously several times. His face was fierce and determined, and his kite well made, with a fine reel.

The boy who had spoken to Young-sup won his match when his opponent stepped out of the circle. The gong sounded to end that match and begin the next. Young-sup walked onto the field. His stomach felt a little peculiar and his head a little light. Later he would barely remember getting to the circle—somehow he was just there, holding his kite and reel and awaiting the signal to launch. He and his opponent bowed to each other, and the match began.

Launching the kite with its ground-pottery line had proved a bit tricky. Because of the danger of getting cut, Young-sup had to use extra care when he threw the kite into the air. But the hours of practice repaid him, and his launch now was flawless.

As the dragon kite rose, the sunlight illuminated its gold-washed scales. The glowing color and the fact that it seemed to fly without a line drew murmurs from the crowd. Young-sup smiled to himself. The King's blue line was indeed difficult to see against the blue of the sky.

Young-sup maneuvered his line and glanced at his

opponent's kite. It was moving into position to bump his own.

The start of each of the preceding matches had followed a similar pattern. The fliers had concentrated on getting a sense of the wind and their opponent's skill and strategy, and there had been little fighting in the first few minutes. Young-sup knew that this match would be different.

He positioned his kite just below his opponent's. Then, holding the reel in both hands, he rapidly drew in some line. The tightening of the line caused the kite to rise quickly. As it rose, the line crossed that of his opponent's and rubbed against it.

The boy glanced quickly at Young-sup; it was unusual for a flier to attempt a line cut so early in the match. Besides, the technique was difficult to execute. The strategy meant that Young-sup's kite was at all times very near and below the opposing kite and might easily be knocked down. The opponent was looking for such an opportunity and did not move his kite away.

The dragon kite rose and fell, obeying the commands of the line as Young-sup reeled in and released, reeled in and released. He counted to himself. Two times, three, four . . .

On the fifth try he made the cut. As the other kite broke free of its line, the dragon kite jerked and seemed to watch it fly away.

Young-sup stole a quick look at his opponent. The boy stood in shock, with his reel trailing a limp line. For a moment Young-sup felt a twinge of guilt when he saw the depths of surprise and unhappiness on his opponent's face.

The match had been won and lost in less than a minute.

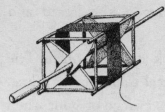

chapter fourteen

When the crowd recovered from its surprise, shouts and applause broke out for the first line cut of the day. Meanwhile, dozens of small boys waited at the far end of the park, downwind of the competition field. As the losing kite sailed off, the stampede began as each raced to be first to reach the kite and claim it for his own.

The gong sounded; Young-sup and his opponent bowed again, first to each other and then toward the King's platform. Young-sup dared not meet the King's eyes for fear of somehow giving away their secret alliance.

He returned to his place in line to watch the other matches. The second line cut of the competition was achieved by Kim Hee-nam. He used a similar technique to Young-sup's, but it took several tries before his opponent's line was severed.

Young-sup's next two matches were nearly identical to his first. The striking appearance of the dragon kite combined with the swiftness of its victories had the crowd buzzing with excitement. With each match the row of contestants grew shorter. With each match the champion stood closer to Young-sup in the line.

....

After Young-sup's third quick victory in a row, the judges conferred briefly, then called him to the platform.

Young-sup told himself he had no reason to feel nervous. He reached the platform and bowed before the judges. The tallest judge, seated in the middle, returned his bow and spoke.

"Your line cuts are most impressive, young flier. We are all agreed that we have never before seen such an efficient display." Young-sup bowed again.

The judge continued, "We have been wondering if it is skill alone that enables you to cut your opponents' lines so easily."

With trembling fingers, Young-sup unreeled some of the line and held it before him. He forced himself to speak clearly, for he did not wish to appear to be hiding anything.

"The part of the line that you see here, Honorable Judges—it has been specially treated. It has been rolled in a mixture of glue and powdered pottery. It is this mixture that stiffens my line and gives it an extra cutting edge."

The judge gestured to a nearby guard, who took the kite and reel from Young-sup and brought them to the judges for closer inspection. The judges examined the line carefully, touched it gingerly, and whispered to one another.

Young-sup held his breath. The old kite seller had said it was not against the rules, but the three judges might still decide against him. It seemed like a long time before they handed the kite back to the guard again.

"We are agreed," the tall judge proclaimed, "that there is nothing in the rules that prohibits the use of such a line. We are also agreed that it would be unfair to make a rule about it now, with the competition already half over. Next year it may be a different story."

The judge paused and looked down at Young-sup. "The final thing that we are agreed on is that the cleverness of this line is matched only by the skill of the one using it." He nodded and bowed. "Fight on, young flier."

Young-sup took the kite from the guard and bowed his thanks. As he walked away, he felt wobbly and realized that his legs had been shaking like the leaves of a willow in the wind.

··

All eyes were on Young-sup as he entered the circle for his fourth match. The crowd, the judges, and Young-sup himself expected another swift victory.

But something wasn't right. He used the same technique as before, but after several attempts the opponent's line still held.

Young-sup tightened and released the line so his kite gained some height and was clear of the battle for a moment. What could be wrong? Was he doing something differently? There was no doubt that this opponent, having also survived three rounds, was highly skilled. Even now his kite was moving in for another attack.

Young-sup tried again. He released some line; feeling the slack, the dragon drifted back, its line rubbing the opponent's. The enemy kite seemed to duck like a boxer, with the other boy trying hard to accomplish the dual feat of avoiding Young-sup's line while knocking his kite. Finally, after two more hard-fought encounters, the opponent's line was frayed to a mere hair. And then the wind joined the fight on Young-sup's side, with a strong gust snapping the kite free.

Young-sup, suddenly exhausted, reeled in his kite. He picked it up and went back to stand in line yet again. On the way there he saw Kee-sup hurrying to his side.

"What's the matter?" Kee-sup asked anxiously. "What happened?"

Young-sup shook his head. "I don't know. I did the same as before—"

"Let me see." Kee-sup took the kite and reel and inspected them. "Look."

He was staring at the section of line that had been coated with the ground pottery. "It's nearly gone."

The glue mixture had worn away with each successive fight. Now there was hardly any of it left on the line, just a few rough patches here and there.

Young-sup looked frightened. "I never thought it might wear off."

"Neither did I."

"What now?"

Kee-sup spoke calmly. "What do you mean, what now? It's no different—you go out there and fly. Just do the best you can. You can win—even without the special line."

Young-sup tried to smile at his brother's reassurance, but inside he felt a quick flame of anger. *He's not the one who's flying,* he thought.

The knock-out contest was down to just four boys. If Young-sup won his next match, he would fight for the championship.

....

To the great surprise of both brothers the semifinal match was as easy as the first three had been. Once again it took only a few maneuvers to sever the opponent's line.

Kee-sup was waiting when Young-sup walked off the field. "What happened this time?"

Together, the brothers bent over the line. There were spots where the glue-and-pottery mixture still clung to the silk, a finger's width here and there. One of these spots must have made contact in the battle.

But all along the once-coated section, the sky-blue silk was beginning to fray.

Young-sup tested it, pulling tentatively at the weak spots. "It will probably hold—there's only one match to go. And if it does, those last little bits might be enough to help me cut his line."

Kee-sup shook his head. "It's not worth the risk. You need to get rid of all that weakened line and retie your reel."

"I need the special line, brother! This next match—it's Kim Hee-nam I'll be fighting."

"You don't need it. You can win without it."

"Against the others, maybe, but not him!"

Kee-sup took the kite and reel and laid them carefully on the ground. He began to untie the fraying line from the kite.

"I'm the one who's flying!" Young-sup protested. "Leave the line alone!"

Kee-sup shook his head and paused in his work to look up at him.

"You have to trust me, little brother. I know what you can do with a kite—even better than you do yourself. And do you know why?" Kee-sup grinned as he cut away the ragged part of the blue silk line. "Because you've never seen yourself fly."

....

As Young-sup reluctantly helped Kee-sup tie the last of the knots to secure the blue line once again, a shadow fell across the kite. The brothers looked up to see their father standing there.

They rose slowly and stood before him. He nodded. "The kite is well made."

Kee-sup bowed. "Yes, Father."

"And so far it has been well flown."

He has been watching, Young-sup thought. "I have done my best, Father."

"But you are not yet finished."

"No, Father. This last round . . ." Young-sup groped for words. "It's Kim Hee-nam. He has twice been the champion before."

His father shrugged, almost imperceptibly. He gestured for Kee-sup to join him. Young-sup took the kite from his brother and watched as they moved toward the crowd. Then his father turned back for a brief moment.

"You are a Lee," he said. "Honor the name."

chapter fifteen

The gong sounded for the final match. Kim Hee-nam strode out onto the field, his head steady and his face calm. As Young-sup tottered out behind him, his insides were boiling and freezing at the same time, and the terror he felt seemed to be screaming out with every step he took.

His brother was watching. His father was watching. The King was watching. The judges . . . the guards . . . the crowd of thousands . . . Young-sup's mind whirled back to the moment when Kee-sup had cut and cast away the last bit of treated line. It was as if he had thrown away Young-sup's chances of victory as well.

The judges gave the signal to launch. Suddenly Young-sup felt as though his body were pushing his confused and frightened mind aside. *You watch,* said his arms and legs and hands, *we know how to do this.*

....

It was true. Young-sup felt as though his mind had gone to sleep, or was just watching, while his body made all the familiar, much-practiced motions on its own. Side by side, almost simultaneously, the red dragon kite and the plain white one rose into the air.

The white kite attacked immediately, its flier wasting no time. It knocked fiercely at the dragon kite.

The dragon dodged and twirled, its scales flashing in the sun. It dipped below the white kite and drew closer in its first attempt to cut the line.

The white kite swung away and hovered just out of reach, as if teasing the dragon to follow it. But the dragon had found a favorable patch of sky and wind and remained where it was. *Patience,* the kite seemed to whisper. *Wait here.*

The white kite charged again, and this time it bumped the dragon. The attack continued, with the white kite knocking the dragon lower and lower and following each time for another hit.

He's not going for a line cut, thought Young-sup. *He's trying to make me crash instead.* Rapidly he loosened the line. The crowd gasped as the dragon seemed to feel the extra slack and veered out of control.

But the slack was what the dragon needed to turn in a new direction. It now had room to find a fresh burst of wind, and it recovered from its dive, climbing higher and higher until once again it flew proudly level with the white kite.

Again and again the white kite attacked, tipping and bumping the dragon. Again and again the dragon recovered. Young-sup had no idea how long they had been flying. It was all he could do to keep his kite from crashing. He was reaching the end of his strength.

....

As Young-sup turned in his struggle to keep the dragon aloft, he caught a glimpse of his brother out of the corner of his eye; Kee-sup had pushed his way through the crowd to the edge of the field.

Enough. A voice came to Young-sup from some-where—from where? Was it the wind or the kite, talking to him? Was it the *tok-gabi* again? *Enough of this. It's time, you know. Cut his line—you can do it, no one better. You've never seen yourself fly.*

It's Kee-sup, Young-sup thought. *He's right here with*

me—he's talking to me somehow. And his strength came back to him as he remembered that more than anyone else it was his brother who deserved his best efforts now.

Young-sup reeled in a little line; the dragon responded to the increased tension by climbing higher. It was now above the white kite. Then he released some length and the dragon drifted back, its line dragging against the opponent's.

Once, twice, three times . . . The white kite moved sideways, trying to escape. Four, five, six. Young-sup could hardly feel where his hands ended and the reel began. Line in, the dragon rose. Line out, the dragon fell. Each time the kite lines crossed and rubbed.

Young-sup shifted his feet as the dragon followed the white kite. Seven, eight, nine. *Surely his line must be frayed.*

Just a few times more . . . Young-sup's whole body leaned and strained, every fiber of his being intent on the battle in the sky. Ten, eleven . . .

The twelfth attempt, and then a gust of wind.

Young-sup lost his balance and fell to his knees outside the circle just as the white kite snapped free.

The soldier's red flag shot up into the air. Pandemonium broke loose. Everyone was shouting.

"The line broke first!"

"No! He fell out of the circle first!"

"It happened at the same time—the very same moment! I saw it!"

The judges had risen at once and were standing in a tight group on the platform. Young-sup staggered to his feet. Above him the dragon kite still flew, unconcerned about the madness below. Automatically Young-sup began to reel it in.

Next to him his opponent was also reeling in—an empty, kiteless line. Kim Hee-nam strode off immediately, without the customary closing bow.

Bewildered, Young-sup picked up the dragon and stood uncertainly in the middle of the field. What would happen now?

A guard from the platform hurried onto the field. He beckoned the soldier with the red flag who had signaled Young-sup's fall out of the circle. The soldier trotted to the platform to speak with the judges.

From a distance Young-sup tried to read their conversation. The soldier was shaking his head, *No.* What did that mean? *No,* the line wasn't cut in time? Or *No,* he hadn't seen what happened?

The noise from the crowd was rising. Excited spectators, jostling and arguing about the result, pushed against the soldiers along the edge of the field. Young-sup searched the crowd for Kee-sup and his father, but the faces seemed to blur into a mass of shouting and confusion and noise.

Someone in the crowd started to chant. "Kim . . . Kim . . . Kim . . ." Other voices joined in, a few at a time.

Everyone knows his name, Young-sup thought.

Kim . . . Kim . . . Kim . . . Kim . . . More people joined in; the chant grew to a roar. KIM! KIM! KIM! It seemed to Young-sup that every single person in the park was shouting his opponent's name.

He had never felt so alone.

Then, from somewhere in the crowd, Young-sup heard something else. Between the incessant beats of KIM . . . KIM . . . KIM, a single voice was chanting a different name.

KIM . . . Lee . . . KIM . . . Lee . . . KIM . . . Lee . . .

Young-sup could hardly believe his ears. The voice was small, but he recognized it at once. Young-sup knew his father must be shouting at the top of his lungs to make himself heard.

Another voice joined in—Kee-sup's.

KIM—Lee—KIM—Lee—KIM—Lee . . .

Lee. A whisper seemed to run through the crowd. *The other fighter's name is Lee.*

And a few at a time, voices added to the strength of the name until both resounded equally through the park.

KIM!

LEE!

KIM!

LEE!

KIM!

LEE!

Young-sup looked around in amazement. The blur of the crowd seemed to clear, and his eyes found Kee-sup again. Then he saw their father push through the crowd to stand at the front, some distance from Kee-sup.

KIM LEE KIM LEE KIM LEE . . .

The chant, almost a song now, had somehow broken the tension in the crowd. People were laughing and shaking their fists good-naturedly at each other as each group tried to outshout the other.

Young-sup caught his brother's eye. He nodded in their father's direction.

And for a moment amid the noise of the shouts and the crowd, their three gazes met. It was then that the brothers saw the rarest of sights: a broad smile on their father's face, as he continued to shout their name.

....

The shouting had been born and grown in only a few moments. Young-sup looked again at the platform. This time he saw Kim Hee-nam approaching the judges.

I should go there, too, thought Young-sup. *I should tell my side of the story.*

But what *was* his side? He could not say clearly that the line had been cut before he fell out of the circle. *I cut the line, and then I fell*, he thought. *No, I fell as I was cutting the line . . .*

He did not know which had happened first.

If that is the truth, he thought, *then that is what I must say.*

Young-sup walked toward the platform. He saw that his opponent had finished speaking to the judges, who were now consulting with the King. A gong sounded, and the chanting crowd was suddenly stilled.

In dead silence, Kim Hee-nam walked back to meet him. Every face in the crowd was turned toward the center of the field. No one spoke; no one even seemed to breathe.

The gong sounded once more, its echoes merging with the blood pounding in Young-sup's ears. Then, to his astonishment, the other boy dropped to his knees in the deepest of bows.

The sudden roar that erupted from the crowd seemed to shake the very earth he stood on.

Young-sup had won.

He was the new champion.

chapter sixteen

Young-sup stood in shock, not knowing what to say.

Kim Hee-nam rose and spoke. "The line broke first. I know, because I felt it, and then I looked at you—just in time to see you fall. I told the judges. It was only fair."

Young-sup heard his words with one part of his mind. Another part was thinking, *Why, he sounds ordinary—just like any other boy. Somehow I imagined that he would be different—prouder or fiercer, perhaps.*

"We haven't met before. I'm Kim Hee-nam. You're a great flier. We should fly together sometime."

Suddenly Young-sup found his tongue. "I'm Lee Young-sup. I'd like that."

Hee-nam smiled. "By the way, what was going on in those first few rounds? I've never seen line cutting like that."

Young-sup laughed. "I'll tell you about it. It was my brother's idea . . ."

And the champions, new and old, walked off the field together.

....

Young-sup sat with his father and brother to observe the men's competition. It felt like years since he had thought of anything but flying, and he was startled to find himself ravenous. He ate enormously of the picnic lunch his father had brought. Seeing his appetite, his father stopped a passing sweet seller and bought several rice cakes.

"Slow down!" Kee-sup complained happily. "That's your third sweet, and I'm still on my first."

Young-sup grinned. It was wonderful to sit there with his mouth full of delicious food, watching the matches between the adult fliers. As well as he and the other boys had flown, he could tell that it would be many years before they would match the skill he was seeing now.

....

The final match ended with a line cut and a tremendous roar from the crowd. Now the King would speak to close the festival. It was over and would not come again for a whole year.

Dusk was falling as the gong sounded and the King rose; the crowd bowed on their knees.

"Rise, my countrymen," said the King, and as he spoke, the shouters began their work again. "I feel great pride today—pride in our traditions, pride in those who were brave enough to compete and those who came to support them. May our land and its traditions live for a thousand years!"

The people shouted their approval. The King waited for the applause and shouts to die down, then continued. "We were all fortunate today to see the best in kite flying. I bow to all those who competed, and especially to this year's champions. Lee Young-sup, winner of the boys' competition, and Ahn Sang-hee, winner of the men's, would you do me the honor of joining me here on the platform?"

Young-sup ducked his head shyly; all around him people were nodding and smiling at him. Some called out brief congratulations to his father. Kee-sup grinned, clapped Young-sup on the back, and gave him a shove toward the platform. Young-sup almost shoved him back but stopped himself. Instead, he bowed his head.

"Older brother, I thank you. I could not have achieved this victory without your assistance." A little wave of surprise washed over Young-sup as he realized that he had spoken to his brother so respectfully not just because their father was present. The words had come unbidden because they were true.

Kee-sup nodded in reply, looking pleased and embarrassed. And as Young-sup turned away and walked to the platform, he felt his father's pride and approval like a warm breeze.

Young-sup stepped up to bow before the King. The King looked at him quickly, their secret friendship dancing in his eyes. Young-sup knew they would meet again soon, when he and Kee-sup returned the dragon kite to its rightful owner. And, he hoped, many times after that.

He stood on one side of the King, with the men's winner on the other.

"No warrior ever fights alone," the King said, "and neither did these two fighters. However great their skills, they could not have achieved what they did today without help."

As the King's words reached them via the shouters, the crowd buzzed and murmured in puzzlement. Young-sup wondered if perhaps the King were about to reveal their partnership.

"And so," the King continued, "I now also honor those who helped them. The valiant dragon of the boys' competition was made by Lee Kee-sup. And Kite Seller Chung made the splendid fish that honored the men's competition. I request that both of these great artists join us here."

Young-sup wanted to shout for joy. Kee-sup and the old kite seller mounted the platform and stood beside their fliers. All four of them bowed to the King and to one another.

Kite Seller Chung nodded at Young-sup. "Well met, young flier." Then he turned to Kee-sup. "The dragon is truly a work of art. It is a kite I would be proud to call one of my own."

Kee-sup bowed again. Young-sup felt a warm glow all through him on seeing his brother at his side—a glow as red and gold as the dragon's scales.

The King continued his speech.

"I wish you all to recall the old story of the great general Kim Yu-sin. A thousand years ago, when he fought against a foreign invasion, his warriors saw a shooting star in the skies. As you know, my people, a shooting star is a very bad omen. The general's troops were discouraged. They felt sure they would lose the coming battle.

"But Kim Yu-sin was as clever as he was brave. He made a very special kite. To this kite he fastened a small lantern. He flew the kite that night, and his soldiers thought that the light was a new star in the sky. A good omen! With their spirits renewed, they won the next day's battle and defeated the invaders."

The crowd cheered wildly. The old story was a great favorite, especially on such a day.

As the King was speaking, two hundred soldiers had been quietly dispersing themselves throughout the park, two by two. One soldier in each pair held a kite, and they waited now for their King's command.

"I close this year's kite festival with a special ceremony. In honor of all kite fliers and kite makers, may our ancestors smile upon you until we meet again next year." Young-sup realized that this was why the King had opened the festival with the wishing kites; he had something else, something new, planned for the closing.

Guards stepped forward and gave small kites to the King, to Kee-sup and Young-sup, and to the kite seller and his flier. Each kite had a tiny lantern attached to one of the crosspieces. The guards lit the lanterns, and one of them helped the King launch his kite.

The crowd watched as the kite rose and faded into the darkening sky, until only its lantern light showed. Then the gong sounded. The soldiers who were scattered among the crowd launched their lantern kites to follow the King's.

Young-sup helped his brother launch, watching until Kee-sup's kite was well on its way. Then he released his own latern kite. It was the last to join the silent fleet in the sky.

Young-sup looked out over the crowd for a moment. Thousands of faces, as far as he could see, were turned skyward. Then he, too, looked up.

More than a hundred lantern lights glowed in the heavens, like stars that were almost close enough to touch. They floated, drifted, sometimes clustered together. Young-sup stared hard, trying to make out which lantern light was on the end of his line.

He gave the line a gentle tug. Far overhead one of the lanterns bobbed and winked in response.

Young-sup smiled, sure now of the light that was his own.

author's note

The boy-King in this story is based on an actual historical figure. King Songjong ruled Korea from 1469 to 1494. The *Sillok,* the official transcript of court activity, records that one of Songjong's acts as King was to mandate that junior ministers were free to voice their opinions to the court, even if their ideas conflicted with those of their superiors.

The use of the colored kite line comes from an observation made by Stewart Culin in the late nineteenth century. In his book *Korean Games,* Culin says that royal kites were flown on a sky-blue line.

It is not known if the use of ground pottery or glass on kite lines originated in Korea; China and India also lay claim to the discovery of this technique. In modern competition the rules are always clear as to whether glass line can or cannot be used. Today's kite fighters coat several different sections of their lines so they always have a fresh cutting edge.

With the modernization of Korea in the twentieth century, Western ideas and culture have taken their place alongside the old Korean ways. Some of the Confucian teachings, such as ancestor worship, have declined in popularity with the spread of Christianity. But other traditions have proved more resistant to change. In most Korean families today the first-born son still bears the responsibility of maintaining the family name and honor, while to some extent the other sons must make their own way in the world.